Synnr's Spark

Zulir Warrior Mates

Kate Rudolph

About the Book

A human born Synnr...
Raised by a Synnr father and human mother, but 100% human, Grace has a foot in two worlds and belongs in neither. A Synnr Match would give her the wings she desperately wants, so why has a human man caught her eye? She's caught between Zac, a human rescued from enemy Apsyns and their evil experiments, and Crowze, an aristocratic Synnr soldier built for seduction. There's no way she can choose between them. So why not choose both?

Lost in space and time...
Zac's supposed to be in grad school, not outer space. He's determined to carve out a life for himself, but he never imagined a three way romance between himself, an alien soldier, and a human woman with the heart of a Synnr warrior.

He'll do what it takes to keep them...
Grace caught his eye through her resilience as a Synnr spy, Zac did it through his will to survive the horrors thrown at him by the Apsyns. Crowze is determined to convince them to take a chance on building something together. But can two humans and a Zulir make a Match?

The Synnrs and Apsyns are on the brink of war in book three of the Zulir Warrior Mates series and Grace, Zac, and Crowze are right in the middle of the action in this MMF alien romance!

Also in this series

Synnr's Saint

Emily was a normal law student until she was abducted by aliens. Forced to perform death defying feats by night and undergoing medical tests by day, she doesn't know how much longer she can take it. When one alien takes particular interest in her she's afraid things have gone from bad to worse. He's got wings and fangs, and he makes her heart pound. But she can't want an alien like that... can she?

Synnr's Hope

Lena is supposed to be back on Earth, but any chance of returning home was stolen by the aliens who kidnapped her. She's safe from those pirates now, but she's going crazy on Aorsa with nothing to do. Her only hope lies with Solan, the smokin' hot military leader responsible for rescuing her from her former captors. She'll team up with him to earn her wings—literally—but no matter what, they're not falling in love.

Chapter One

What was Grace doing here?

It was Emily and Oz's bonding ceremony.

She wasn't a friend of either Emily or Oz, and in fact, she was pretty sure that Emily hated her. She couldn't blame the earthling. They had met under less than stellar circumstances: being experimented on and tortured by the sadistic Apsyns down on Kilrym, with Grace playing the part of Apsyn-lover.

But that's what happened when you were a spy. Sometimes you had to treat the people you were trying to save like *braz*.

Grace hadn't been planning to come. She'd been surprised to receive an invitation, and she'd told her mother in passing. But it was her mother who said she should go. Her mother, who pointed out she didn't have a lot of friends anymore.

Or that she had never had friends in the first place.

Grace didn't need to be reminded. She'd grown up a human-born Synnr with one foot in both worlds. Her blood was completely human, something she wished wasn't true every day. But the only father she'd ever known was a Synnr, and her mother had lived on Aorsa for the past twenty-five years. It was home. Even if Grace would never completely fit in.

The bonding ceremony ended while Grace was lost in her thoughts. Emily and Oz were looking at each other with love in their eyes and weren't paying any attention to the rest of the guests. Grace could make her escape. No one would notice. She looked down at her timepiece and promised herself that she could take off in ten more minutes. That was it. She just had to survive ten minutes. She had survived torture and the Apsyns. Ten minutes at a bonding ceremony was nothing.

"They look really happy, don't they?" a skinny blonde girl asked. Luci. The young one. Grace had thought the girl was afraid of her, but most of that fear had dissolved once they made it safely out of Apsyn custody.

"It's nice," Grace replied. What else was she supposed to say? It was a bonding ceremony. Was she supposed to insult one of the bond mates? Say that their Match would never last? No, she wasn't rude. Luci stared at her for several long moments before finally turning around and walking away without saying another word.

Grace wanted to curse. She was supposed to be *nice*. She was supposed to be trying to prove that these humans had nothing to fear from her. So why couldn't she do it?

She was human. As much as it frustrated her. Her mother was from Earth. She had a biological father from Earth, not that she knew his name or anything about him. She wasn't technically a Synnr. She wasn't Zulir. So why couldn't she make friends with these *punting* humans?

She sensed someone come up behind her and glanced over, expecting to see Luci returning. But it wasn't Luci.

Crowze.

A Synnr soldier and aristocrat who was wearing a tight suit like it was made for him. Of course, given his wealth, it probably was. Her eyes flicked up and down as she appreciated the look of him.

His hair was dark and cropped short, his skin iridescent with blue undertones. His tattoos peeked out from under the sleeves of his jacket. Not bonding tattoos. Not like Emily and Oz. She didn't know what they looked like, but she wanted to push his sleeve up and see.

She wouldn't. She wasn't crazy.

Attracted. But not crazy.

She'd been thinking about him a lot in the few weeks since she had arrived back on Aorsa with him and his crew and all of the humans they'd rescued from Kilrym. She hadn't done anything about it, of course. He was a Synnr aristocrat. She was just a human.

Her mother would kill her if she caught her having thoughts like that. Ever since Grace had been a little girl, her mom had insisted that she was just as good as all the Synnrs around them. There was no difference. So what if they could summon wings with a thought and zap their enemies with electricity?

Grace had tricks of her own. Allegedly.

But that didn't mean she was about to start up something with the Synnr aristocrat. Sure, she wanted a Synnr Match. She had submitted her biological data to the Matching Bureau as soon as she was old enough to do so. She would jump at the chance for a Match, aristocrat or no. But it concerned her when Synnrs seemed to be interested. Some of them had strange obsessions with humans, and she didn't want to be the object of anyone's fetish.

So where did Crowze fall?

He seemed to like humans, that was true enough. He had allowed all of the humans that they had rescued from Kilrym to settle on his estate. He didn't have to do that. Someone would've found a place for them. But a month later the humans were still there, and she had never heard him complain or mention that one day they would be leaving. Was it kindness? Fetish? Or something even darker?

Perhaps Grace should give him the benefit of the doubt. But optimism had been ripped away after spending six months embedded in Apsyn territory. She slowly recovered her sense of self in the last month, but when things got bad she could feel her mind slipping into the shady places she'd been forced to hide when trying to ingratiate herself with the Apsyns. She hadn't crossed any line she couldn't come back from, but she knew the other humans thought she had done dark and terrible things.

"That's not the look anyone should have at a bonding ceremony," said Crowze, the smooth tones of his aristocratic accent sliding over her and making her shiver.

Grace didn't immediately shift her features back to something pleasant. Reacting swiftly to a person's comment was a quick way to break character in the field, and she didn't break. But after a few seconds, the corner of her mouth tugged up into a pleasant smile. "Is there a law?"

"Would a law make you happy?" Crowze asked. He was close enough that she could feel the heat of his body and smell his woodsy, masculine scent.

Soap? Perfume? She wasn't going to ask, but the smell was imprinted on her senses, and she knew if she caught a whiff anywhere else, she would think of him. "Are you so concerned with my happiness?"

"Frighteningly so." The seductive edge of his words slipped for a moment and Grace almost believed he was telling the truth. The look on his face made her want to do things she'd regret.

Was this more than idle flirtation? She couldn't get caught up. Nothing would come of it. The world was on the edge of war and she didn't have time for a relationship. Not unless it was with her Match.

But would one night of fun hurt?

"Dance with me." His words hovered between question and a command, and before she knew it,

Grace found herself in Crowze's embrace. They weren't in the main area of the party, instead in a secluded path surrounded by shrubs and trees. If it had been dark out it would've been romantic, but the sun didn't set at this time of the year on Aorsa.

Grace swayed with Crowze, letting him take the lead. He was good, guiding her through the motions without ever making it seem like it took effort. She could get lost like this. Could get addicted to it.

Maybe one night was too much.

"I hoped I'd have the pleasure," Crowze said, his breath whispering against her ear. "I've wanted you in my arms." He pressed close and she could feel *all* of him. Or she imagined she did. What would it feel like if the clothes came off?

"I bet you say that to all the humans." It was a little too caustic to be flirtatious, but Grace couldn't help herself. The real her, the girl she had to forget when she was playing a part, wasn't sweet, or docile, or forgiving. She was tough and a bit rough. There was a reason she didn't have many friends.

But Crowze didn't take it personally. "I didn't ask you to dance because you're human." And he didn't seem to mind that she was… prickly.

"You didn't?" She wanted to believe it. But if there was anyone she knew that she could accuse of being obsessed with humans, it was Crowze. Why else would he keep so many so close?

Why would he look at her so intensely?

"No." He squeezed her for a moment before sliding his hands down her sides to rest on her hips.

"Then why?" Grace didn't like the breathy tone, but she couldn't help herself. This felt too good. She had to get away. But she didn't want to leave.

One dance. She was allowed to have one magical dance.

"Because I can't stop thinking about you." His fingers dug into her hips, not enough to hurt, but they kept her in place. Grace knew a dozen moves to get out of his embrace, but she didn't want out. She liked the feel of his raw power, and she didn't think she was imagining the lightning of his spark that danced in his eyes.

She knew he was going to kiss her. She read the intention as clear as day, and she didn't back up or back down.

And when his lips found hers, she couldn't stifle the moan. He tasted like a dream, like a promise she didn't know he was making. She could kiss him all night and never get enough of it, and that thought scared her.

Grace tore her lips away from him and stepped back. Crowze opened his mouth and made a sound, but she turned around and took off before he could say anything else. She had to get away before she did something stupid.

Then Grace had to wonder what was really so stupid about starting something with Crowze. If he was her Match he'd be everything she wanted.

She meant to head to her vehicle, but ended up running deeper into the hedges that formed a small maze in the center of the property. She wasn't exactly sure where she was, but she didn't panic. Her mind was still racing and she needed to calm down. She stopped running and found herself in a nice alcove.

"Are you okay?" The voice startled her, but Grace didn't jump. She turned around smoothly and saw Zac Hale standing there. He was one of the humans she'd helped rescue from Kilrym a month before. He had floppy dark blond, almost brown hair and extremely pale skin. If she were close she knew she'd see the fine veins running blue under the surface. He also had a promising definition to his muscles that she'd noticed and admired.

She'd admired a lot of him. And then she'd cursed herself for doing so. He was *human*. He could never be her Match. And she'd been doing her best to put him out of her mind.

She didn't want to bond with a human; she wanted wings, wings that only a Synnr could give her.

Maybe she should run back and see if she could find Crowze.

But Zac didn't see her turmoil. He was waiting there, a cautious smile on his face. He knew her well enough by now to know she was just as likely to lash out as not when asked to engage in polite conversation. "I'm fine," she said. It was true. It was always true. One little kiss wasn't enough to throw her off, and neither was a stupid crush that didn't seem to be going anywhere.

"Are you hiding?" he asked. There wasn't any accusation in his voice, and if he was in this maze, then he might have been hiding too.

A small bench sat a few steps away, just big enough for two people. Grace sank down onto it and after half a moment Zac sat beside her. "I think I've had enough bonding for today," Grace confessed. Emily and Oz were disgustingly in love, and if she hung around much longer, watching them would make her sick to her stomach.

"Have you been to many of these?" Zac asked. The bench was small enough that she could absorb his body heat like a caress. It wasn't the same as Crowze. Crowze had set out to dance with her, to kiss her, to seduce her. She didn't think Zac was doing the same. Then again, she didn't know how humans approached liaisons on Earth.

Was he playing a game? Or was he being the friendly man she had come to know over the past month? "A few." And every time she came to one of the ceremonies, she was reminded that she had no Match for herself. She hadn't cared when she was young. And she realized that twenty-five wasn't exactly old, but she was tired of waiting. It was too bad there was nothing she could do about it.

Zac seemed to sense some part of what she was feeling and was kind enough to change the subject. "I was thinking about what kind of tattoo I want. How about a giant dragon?" He ran his hand up and down the sleeve of his jacket, right where a bonding tattoo would go.

Despite herself, Grace laughed. "I don't think it works like that."

His grin was sweet enough to make her heart clench. There was something about Zac.

If only he was a Synnr.

"Maybe if I think really hard it will work. I'll focus on having black scales, bright fire, and giant ass wings." His eyes were bright with excitement.

"Well, you would have the wings." Electric wings, blues and reds and greens. Grace wanted to know what hers would look like. And for a moment she could imagine Zac with wings of his own. Blue would work well for him with strands of bright green braided through. They would be beautiful.

And Grace hated them. Because if he had wings it meant that he had a Match. That he was with someone other than her. Not that a relationship between them was an option. Not when she wanted wings of her own.

She hadn't ever wished that she'd been born on Earth before. But maybe that would've been easier. Maybe then she could have met a nice man like Zac and never had to wonder what things would be like on an alien planet where neither of them quite belonged.

"We're talking about the cool tattoo," Zac said, knocking her out of her sullen reverie. "Come on. What would you have?"

Was that really all this was to him? Didn't he care about the wings? Didn't he care about fitting in? What must that be like? Then again, he had only been among the Zulir for a matter of months. He didn't have an entire lifetime of feeling different. "I've never thought of it that way," she said. She wanted the wings. A bonding tattoo was something optional. Something she didn't really care about.

Weren't the wings sign enough that she was Matched?

"There's got to be something," Zac insisted. If it were someone else she would've walked away. But somehow Zac's insistence didn't bother her. She didn't know why.

Stupid crush. Stupid men.

Grace thought hard. Though many Synnrs started tattooing themselves at a young age, Grace had never done so. Nothing had ever meant enough to her. But if she had to choose, what would it be?

Well, there was *one* thing she wanted. "I don't have a specific design in mind, but I guess I want mine to be more complex than my mom's." It was petty but true. Her mother's bonding tattoo was beautiful in its simplicity, a series of lines zigzagging up and down her arm in different shades of blue. Grace wanted swirls. Something curving. Something complicated.

Zac bumped her shoulder with his own. "There you go!"

Grace turned to face him and their eyes met. The smile froze on his face and time stood still as they stared at one another. His eyes flicked down to her lips and his tongue darted out.

He was going to kiss her. She read the intention as clear as day. All she had to do was sit there and let it happen.

She could still taste a faint hint of Crowze on her lips. What would he taste like mixed with Zac?

Zac leaned in an inch.

Grace jumped up from the bench. "I need to go."

***

Zac watched Grace flee and tried not to be disappointed. Had he scared her? Had he read that situation wrong?

He wouldn't call himself an expert, but he thought they were flirting. Everything was different on Aorsa, and he had to remind himself that even though Grace was human, she wasn't from Earth. He didn't want to cross a line. Didn't want to make an unwanted advance.

But there had been desire in her eyes. She'd leaned towards him. He was sure of it.

He had to let the frustration go. She'd been acting weird. And it wasn't just because of the almost kiss.

He would check on her later. See if something was up. As a friend. He didn't need to become her boyfriend to care about her. She was a cool person. And he wanted to be her friend no matter what.

The other humans who he had been rescued with didn't see it, but he did. Grace had a biting sense of humor to go along with the rest of her prickly personality. But she could be kind. She had been giving him and his fellow humans lessons in life on Aorsa for the past month. He didn't think anyone had asked her to do so, but she was taking time out of her day several times a week to teach them about life in their new home.

Of course he wanted to be her friend.

Zac stood up from the bench and looked around. He'd had no trouble finding Grace earlier, but now it looked like he was in the middle of a maze. He wasn't exactly sure which way he had come in, and after turning around twice, he didn't know which way Grace had gone. He didn't have the best sense of direction, but it hadn't been an issue back home. Notre Dame wasn't exactly huge.

With no other choice he chose a path and started walking.

He wished he had some breadcrumbs to lay down. He was afraid the path would lead him to a witch's house and he would end up being eaten. That would be an auspicious end to the crazy journey his life had taken.

The hairs on the back of his neck prickled before Zac turned a corner, and it was abundantly obvious why when a figure came into view. Crowze. A zing of awareness went through Zac.

Now he wasn't worried about being eaten by a witch. Crowze looked ready to devour him.

The man was hot. Sexy, refined, educated, and just a bit dangerous.

He was exactly the kind of guy Zac's mom would have warned him to stay away from… if she had known he was into guys. He hadn't been out to many people back home. When he'd told his best friend in high school that he was bisexual, the guy had accused him of lying, of being selfish, and of having a crush on him.

It taught Zac to be very careful in choosing his friends. Things were better in college. He'd found a boyfriend of his own for a few months. And then a girlfriend. And then he had become so engrossed in his studies that relationships fell by the wayside.

But he wasn't studying anything anymore. And Crowze was *very* hot.

Zac told his cock to calm down. How could he go from flirting with Grace to eyeing Crowze in a matter of minutes? It didn't seem right. But she'd rejected him, a logical part of his brain tried to point out. There was nothing going on between them, he'd made no promises. And he could be reading in to whatever look Crowze was throwing him.

Synnrs weren't homophobic. And it wasn't even the grudging acceptance he'd gotten from some of his friends and colleagues back home. No, here they didn't care at all. Gay, straight, bi, or any other words to describe love, it was all the same to them. They didn't even care if a relationship involved more than two people. It had taken Zac a minute to wrap his mind around that.

And to think, back home in 2007 gay people couldn't even get married.

Not everything about his new world was terrible.

"Are you having a nice time?" Crowze asked, taking a few steps and closing the distance between them.

Zac could feel the heat rising on his cheeks and cursed his pale skin. He had never been able to hide his emotions. His blushes and flushes gave him away every time.

"It's a nice party," he said, voice even. He was proud of himself. He'd felt in control of the conversation when he was talking to Grace, but with one question, Crowze had easily taken the reins of this little flirtation. Conversation. Whatever. Was Crowze even into him? Or was Zac jumping to conclusions?

"This is your first bonding ceremony, isn't it?" Crowze asked. He casually reached out and ran his fingers down Zac's arm.

It was bold, too bold to ignore. But Zac didn't hate it. And he didn't step back. He definitely wasn't making the wrong assumption. "I've only been here a month, haven't had much time for anything else."

Crowze smiled, and Zac wondered if it was the kind of smile the shark gave a fish right before gobbling it up. "True. You've shaken things up."

Now he was confused. "Me?" Zac wasn't anything special, just a boy from Indiana who'd been abducted by aliens.

"You and your humans," said Crowze. "My estate has never been so…"

"Crowded?" Zac suggested.

Crowze laughed, the sound deeper than Zac would've suspected given Crowze's normal tone. "Lively."

Lively was one word for it. Crowze had offered the humans who were rescued from Kilrym the use of one of the houses on his estate. And it was a huge estate. In the last month Zac and his fellow humans had done their best to make the house a home. It wasn't perfect. But it didn't suck.

"I'm sorry for making things difficult." A dozen people suddenly living on a property had to be disruptive, no matter how big the property was.

"Not at all," Crowze insisted. "I wouldn't have invited you if it would be a problem."

"I don't want to take advantage." It felt wrong to take free accommodation like that. Especially when the accommodation was a freaking mansion. But he'd be lying if he said that having a place like Human House hadn't made a rough transition to life on an alien planet a bit easier.

"Am I taking advantage?" Crowze asked. He ran his fingers up Zack's other arm and let them rest on his elbow.

"Huh?" Zac swallowed hard. Crowze was so close that Zac could breathe in the scent of his soap and see the hint of the fangs he had hidden in his mouth. The Zulir appeared mostly human. But then they showed their electric wings, or their fangs, or lightning danced in their eyes, and Zac was reminded just how different they were. How alien.

"I know humans could be... particular," Crowze said, still not backing away.

"What?" Crowze was too close for Zac to think about anything but his presence. His heart was beating fast and he wanted to lean into the Synnr and see how far he could take things.

"About romance," Crowze said.

"Romance?" What were they talking about? Zac was too primed with want to follow it.

"Are you?" Crowze asked. The space between them was disappearing by the second and as far as Zac was concerned that couldn't happen soon enough.

Why weren't they kissing? Seriously, Zac could do with a good make out session right now. And Crowze was right there. "Am I?" Was he what? And then it dawned on him. Crowze was asking about his sexuality in a particularly Synnr fashion. "Oh! No. No particularities here."

And that shark's smile was back. "Good." It sent a zing of desire through Zac and made his cock twitch.

Crowze leaned in close and sealed their mouths together. It was a good kiss. Not too insistent, but not at all timid. Zac opened his mouth, ready for the taste of Crowze's tongue.

"I forgot my... Oh!" It was Grace.

Crowze let go of Zac, but they didn't step apart.

Grace was looking at them, her gaze darting back and forth and her eyes dark with anger. Without another word, she turned around and took off.

"Wait!" Both Zac and Crowze said it and then shared a look. Zac couldn't decipher what Crowze was trying to tell him, but they didn't have time for conversation. They both took off after Grace, but got split up in the maze.

Zac searched for several minutes and he was successful in finding her. Sort of. He made it to the parking lot and saw Grace slide into her vehicle, slam the door, and drive away. He didn't try to chase after her. He wasn't exactly sure what just happened, and he ended the night more frustrated than expected.

Perhaps it was better to end the night alone. He wasn't sure he could handle Synnr romance.

Chapter Two

Crowze wanted to know what in *Braznon's bowels* he'd been thinking.

He'd gotten impatient. If he'd acted like that on the battlefield he would be dead. And what was romance if not a battlefield all its own?

He'd had an eye on Grace for years, ever since she joined the military and their paths crossed. The timing had never been right. It was one long mission after another. But Crowze was coming to realize that the timing would never *be* right. Not with war on the horizon.

And then there was Zac. The human man who had been rescued from Earth, who had escaped Apsyn custody with a handful of human friends. He was a mix of brave and sweet. Not a soldier, but a scholar, and he called to that part of Crowze. The part that couldn't be sated by violence.

He wanted both of them. They complemented each other, and he thought they could complete him.

But with one stupid move he'd ruined it all.

He had never been much for relationships. A few liaisons that went nowhere, where all partners understood what they were there for. It was different than what he wanted now.

Now he wanted something real, something permanent, something like Emily and Oz had. The ache had been growing within him for some time now. He had a vast estate, the responsibilities that came from being the head of his family. But he wanted a home. He wanted a partner. Or, well, *partners*.

He didn't care if he had a Match or not. He had never submitted his name to the Matching database. If it happened, it would happen, and he didn't need someone to test his DNA to find the most compatible person. Where was the magic in that? Matches were supposed to be about fate.

He had to put his romantic woes out of his mind.

There was training to be done with the war coming. The Apsyns had already bombed a military installation and they were bound to escalate their aggression. He didn't know what would come next. He didn't know how long it would be before they received an outright declaration of war. But there was no time to waste.

Crowze made it to the training facility and met Ax outside. He passed Lena in the hall and was surprised to see her. Immediately, guilt twinged at his conscience. He had promised to try and find her a job among the Synnrs, but he hadn't done so yet. She must have made moves of her own if she was training here. And he recalled seeing her with Solan at the bonding ceremony the night before. They had looked very comfortable together. He wondered what was going on there.

That was a question for later. He wasn't going to stop Lena and ask for a bit of gossip.

He and Ax changed into training clothes and made their way to their training station. They warmed up with hand-to-hand combat, playing dirty and throwing tricks at one another. They had known each other since they were boys, and this was a game they had played many times before. The only rule was not to hit the tender bits, anything else was fair game. But it was Ax who had to cry mercy once they were both drenched in sweat when Crowze got him in a particularly nasty arm bar.

"I almost had you," Ax panted. He slicked back his sweat-drenched hair and grabbed his bottle of water, drinking it down in great gulps.

"If you could have had me, you would have." Ax was a great fighter, but he wasn't ruthless enough against his friends. Put him against an Apsyn and there was no mercy. But on the training floor he could always be beaten.

"One day I'll get you," said Ax with determination that Crowze almost believed.

"You wish." Crowze doubted he would ever see that day. And the banter was part of their training.

"Target training?" Ax suggested with a nod toward the door and a gleam in his eye.

"Perfect." As they made their way to a different part of the training facility, Grace came out of another room. She caught sight of Crowze and her eyes narrowed. If she'd had a spark of her own he would be incinerated. Even without the power he felt his skin prickle.

Braznon's bowels. Crowze had messed up. He opened his mouth, ready to apologize or explain, to say *something* that would make her understand what he wanted. But she stormed past him, careful not to get close enough to be caught, before he could say anything.

Ax looked between them and then watched until Grace turned the corner. "What was that all about?" he asked, brows raised in confusion.

Crowze kept quiet until they made it into the target practice room. He didn't want his life and his romantic interests to be gossip fodder, and nothing spread through the facility quicker than personal drama. "We had a moment at the bonding ceremony," he said. That didn't do it justice. He could remember the feel of her body pressed against his, the way they had moved in perfect rhythm to the music. And the taste of her lips.

He wanted more. Wanted to feel her under him. Wanted to feel her pressed against him with Zac at her back. He wanted it all.

"A moment?" Ax looked at him and waited for more.

Did they have to do this? Crowze was too aware of his own failures to speak without hitting something, and he'd already pummeled Ax once today. "There are targets to hit." He turned and started to program his own.

But Ax wasn't letting him get away with that. "A glare like that doesn't come from a single kiss. Unless…" He let the word hang there.

"You know I didn't force her." It made him sick to his stomach to think it. He would never. And he would gut anyone who tried.

Ax let out an annoyed sound. "Of course I know that." He turned and programmed his own target. "So what was it?"

There was no escaping the explanation. It was best to just get it out. "After I kissed her, she found me kissing Zac a few minutes later," Crowze confessed. And that was another experience all to itself. The way Zac had blushed as they stood close together. The way he had been caught between temptation and flight. He knew humans could have different sensibilities about relationships, that they weren't as open-minded as the Zulir, but Zac had been eager. He had wanted it. And Crowze wanted him. And Grace.

"What's the problem with that?" Ax was a sensible Synnr who couldn't understand the delicate situation Crowze was in.

"I didn't think there was one." It had all seemed so obvious to him. The bonding ceremony was a perfect place to test the interest of the people he wanted. "Grace saw me kiss Zac." He didn't want to talk about this, but maybe he needed to.

"Are you saying you kissed them separately? Or together?" Now Ax wasn't paying any attention to his target.

"Separately." His uncles and aunt made this look easy. What was the trick? Should he have sent Zac and Grace some sort of documentation declaring his intent?

"You're saying you did not talk to them before you did this? That you didn't see if they might want something together?" Ax was shaking his head in exasperation.

"No. Should I?" Why was there no handbook for this?

"Yes, you should." He said it like Crowze was a disobedient pet or child, like he should have known better.

Crowze turned to his target. "I'd rather beat your ass at this."

Ax let the subject drop. For now. But Crowze wasn't optimistic that it would stay dropped forever. He wanted Grace and Zac. So how was he going to make that happen?

***

Grace *wasn't* thinking about the night of the bonding ceremony.

Seeing Crowze at the training facility was just about the worst thing she could imagine. The image of him kissing Zac was seared into her mind. A hot stab of jealousy burned deep inside her, and she seethed.

Jealousy? Maybe that wasn't exactly the right word. She hadn't been jealous when she dreamed about the two of them. But now seeing Crowze with Ax, it made her wonder if he was like that with everyone.

Was he kissing Ax in private alcoves too?

Grace stomped out of the building and made her way to her vehicle. She needed to forget about Crowze. Forget about stolen kisses, and Synnr aristocrats, and cute humans. War was coming. Who cared about romance?

She'd thought Crowze had seen something in her. Something special. Maybe he saw something special in both her and Zac. But now he was walking and laughing next to Ax while she was being torn up inside.

Player.

That was what he was. He would go after anything with a heartbeat. And possibly some alluring plants. She didn't need a guy like that.

Or a guy like Zac. No guys. No girls. No one. She was fine by herself.

The drive home didn't take long. She lived close enough to the training facility that her anger had just enough time to boil over into something like rage by the time she was pulling her vehicle into the family garage and slamming the door behind her. She trudged into the house and was happy not to hear the sounds of anyone else.

It was a big house, but not big enough for all the people that lived there. Her, her mother, her father, two uncles, an aunt, her two sisters, and four cousins. Grace hadn't seen any other cars in the garage, but she could hear someone moving around in the kitchen as she got further into the house. She turned a corner and saw her mother standing over the stove and stirring something in a pot.

Grace looked a lot like her mother: the same blonde hair, the same eyes and high cheekbones. It wasn't like she could look like anyone else. She didn't know what her father looked like or even what his name was. Well, that wasn't exactly right. Her *father* was named Romy and he was a Synnr warrior. He just wasn't her biological father.

"You look like you've had a day," said her mother, Valerie, with a sympathetic smile.

"I'm fine." Grace winced as she said it. Nothing about that sounded fine. She sounded like a petulant child. And very clearly not okay. But she *was* fine. She had to be. She wasn't going to let some stupid guy trouble throw her off.

Valerie laughed. "Fine? Take a seat." She nodded towards one of the benches at the counter across from the stove.

Grace climbed up and slumped. She had spent many hours on this bench watching her mother cook. All the kids had. "What are you making?" Whatever it was it smelled delicious.

"Summer stew, and some fresh bread." Her mom gave the pot a final stir and put a lid on it before turning to face Grace. "And you won't get a bite if you don't tell me what's going on."

She played dirty. Summer stew was one of Grace's favorites. Well, Grace had to get it from somewhere. "It's stupid. I thought a guy liked me but it turns out he's just a player."

Valerie's eyes narrowed and her grip tightened on the wooden spoon, like she was ready to wield it for a beat down. "Does he still have all his limbs? The last guy that hurt you—"

Grace groaned. "I was seventeen! And besides, he should've known better." But she didn't want to talk about her first partner. She never wanted to think about that disaster again. "No, this is nothing like that. I just read into something more than I should have." She wanted a Match for forever. Crowze wanted a night.

"Who is this evil player?" Another mom might have afforded her daughter some pity, but Valerie had a bit of a smirk going, as if she were enjoying Grace's pain.

Grace knew she wasn't. At least, she hoped she wasn't. But Grace could count on her hand with fingers to spare the number of times she had complained about romantic troubles. Her mom had to savor the few times it happened. "Someone I work with. Crowze."

"Crowze Ergas?" Valerie scrunched up her face and thought. "I've heard things about him, but never anything about being a player."

"Well he is. It's either that or I'm not Synnr enough for him." Even as she said it she knew it was wrong. First of all, Crowze had been kissing Zac too. Zac, who was even more human than Grace. Second of all, her mother would never let her get away with saying that.

"He *told* you that?" Her eyes darted towards the knives hanging on the wall. Grace held up a hand to keep her mom from going for a weapon.

"No! He didn't say anything like that." She wasn't feeling charitable towards Crowze, but she wasn't about to send her enraged mother after him. Her dad was the warrior, but she had a feeling her mom knew how to hide a body if things got bad.

"You're as much of a Synnr as anyone." It wasn't the first time her mother had said those words, and it wouldn't be the last. She had embraced Synnr life when she met her Match, and she had always insisted that Grace belonged where she was. "If someone can't see that, that's their loss."

But Grace was tired of that pep talk. "I'm human, I'll never *not* be human. No spark. No wings. Not a Synnr." Grace kept that inside as much as she could. It ate her up. But who really understood it? Her mother who had wings from her Match? Her sisters who were half Zulir? Her cousins who were full Zulir?

No one knew what it was like to be her. Not even the humans who'd just been rescued from Kilrym. She had never seen Earth. She knew nothing about it. Not even her father's name.

She belonged nowhere and with no one.

"There's more to being a Synnr than having wings," said Valerie. "Synnrs are loyal to their people, they are strong, they are honest, they are just. You are all of those things. You were raised to be a Synnr. Your father is a Synnr. I am a Synnr. Never forget that."

"And what about a spark?" It was the heart of the Zulir. The thing that gave them their power. The thing that made a Match.

Her mom shook her head. "If you think that's what makes a person a Synnr, then you don't understand at all." Valerie turned away and stared down at the stew.

Grace wanted to get up and leave. This wasn't the first time she'd had this argument with her mother. And every time it left them bruised, right on the edge of broken. She could offer up a peace offering, give her mom some hint of what was going on with Zac or information about her training, and it would make things better in an instant.

But it wouldn't make the heart of their problems go away. She didn't want to fight. Not when the only thing that she could wound was her mother's heart.

And her mother must've felt the same way. "Any changes to the database?" she asked lightly.

She was talking about the database maintained by the Matching Bureau. Grace had submitted her biological information the moment she was old enough to do so. She wanted a Match. Humans might not have been able to access their spark on their own, but something about the Zulir was compatible about them. If she had a Zulir Match she would be able to use her spark, would be able to grow wings. "No changes." She checked at least once a week, sometimes more. The Bureau was supposed to contact her if a compatible Match appeared, but she didn't trust them. Not without checking for herself.

"You'll find something. And if I know you, it won't be the Matching Bureau that's responsible for your bonding. You'll will it into existence on your own."

Was that supposed to be a compliment? Grace knew she was stubborn.

Her mother's communicator beeped and she let out a curse, one of those funny little Earth words that she had never quite let go of, despite having spent the last twenty-five years living among the Zulir. "I have to go into work. Will you keep an eye on this?" she asked, nodding towards the stew. "You'll need to take it off the heat in another hour.

"I can do that. When is the brood getting home?" The stew smelled divine and Grace's stomach growled. She'd be tasting it long before an hour was up.

"Not sure," Valerie said. "Your dad is due home in a couple of hours. I had hoped to see him tonight. But I doubt I'll be in until morning." She stuck her communicator in her pocket and came around the counter to kiss Grace on the forehead. "I'll see you later." And then she was gone.

Now the house was completely silent. Grace enjoyed it for all of thirty seconds before it started to feel weird. Most of her life she was surrounded by other people; whether it was her house, or out on a mission, she was never alone.

For a second she imagined what it would be like if Crowze and Zac were there with her. Together. If she had both of them, she would never need to be alone again. Wouldn't that be nice?

Chapter Three

Grace tasted sweet. Zac groaned as his lips pressed against hers, tongues swiping and bodies tangled together in the silken sheets of his small bed. There was barely enough room for him, but he didn't care.

The soft press of her breasts was enough to make his cock perk up, and he thrust against her, the noise that tore out of his throat inhuman. Her fingers dug into his shoulders, and he was sure he'd be bruised, but he'd wear her marks proudly. What better way to show the world that she belonged to him?

She pulled away and Zac wanted to tug her back. He didn't know if he'd ever get enough of her. Distantly, his mind tried to tell him that he hadn't ever tasted her before, but he shoved the thought away. This was more real than anything.

It was all he wanted.

Was it?

A groaning gasp caught his attention and he turned his head. There was Crowze, sitting in a chair beside the bed, hand wrapped around his cock as he stroked, watching Zac and Grace.

Zac shot up from the bed, the dream clinging to him like a sticky-sweet memory.

Four days after the bonding ceremony and Zac could still feel the press of Crowze's lips against his. He could also remember the scandalized sound that Grace had made when she caught them. It had kept him up at night. Did she have a problem with two men kissing?

Or was it something else?

That wasn't the only question that had made him toss and turn. Every night for four days he'd woken sweat-slicked from dreams of him and Grace and Crowze all in one giant bed, rolling around together with no thought but to bring each other pleasure. Not unlike his nap dream.

That was new. Two partners. Was that what he wanted? Did he want Crowze and Grace together? Or was his mind simply caught between the two and unsure which was the better choice?

He was so caught up in his emotional state that something that should have been fascinating could not hold his attention. He had a book of Synnr fairytales in front of him, and he had been reading the same page for the past ten minutes. Lena had taught all of the humans a trick. At first they hadn't been able to read the Zulir language, but after learning the alphabet, their translators were able to do the rest of the work. He was thankful for it. His entire life he'd been surrounded by books, and he had been dreading being unable to read.

But by the time he had gone to thank Lena, she had disappeared. He didn't know where she was, but since Emily wasn't concerned, Zac didn't think it was anything to be worried about. Apparently she had managed to get a job with the Synnr military. Maybe it was some kind of training mission.

A few minutes later, Joel knocked on his door. Zac let him in and watched as he took a seat in the same chair Crowze had been watching him and Grace from in the dream. He couldn't get caught up in that. Crowze wasn't here. That wasn't real.

They were supposed to be practicing their reading skills in Zac's room. Over the past few weeks he had grown closer to Joel, an older man who had been one of the humans that had escaped with him, Lena, Emily, and Luci.

Zac forced himself to wake up, to forget about the dream and put aside thoughts of Grace and Crowze. It wasn't easy.

"If you sigh any louder you're going to deafen me," said Joel. He closed his book and looked at Zac, one eyebrow raised.

"I'm just thinking," said Zac. Could he tell Joel what the problem was? He wasn't sure exactly what time Joel came from or how judgmental he would be.

Zac had been plucked out of 2007, Lena from 2006, Luci from 2013, and Emily from 2019. They were all close enough in time to have similar points of reference, and then Emily or Luci would say something that seemed completely impossible. How could a handful of years make such a difference?

Joel had never said the specific time he was from, but judging by the way he spoke to everyone, he had to be somewhere in the mix with the rest of them. But he was also older, on the other side of forty, at least. Would he care that Zac was bi? Would he care that Zac was thinking about kissing a man... and a woman? There was only one way to find out. But Zac was terrified to try.

Still, he needed a friend. He needed advice. And Joel was sitting right there.

Zac took a deep breath and let it all out. "Crowze kissed me at Emily and Oz's bonding ceremony. Grace caught us. And I tried to kiss her. Before she caught us," he rushed to correct himself. He didn't want to confuse the order of events. "I'm attracted to both of them. I'm not sure what to do with it." When he said it like that it didn't sound complicated at all. Four sleepless nights and it all came down to a couple sentences.

He had been freaking abducted by aliens, so why was this his most pressing concern?

Well, he was safe from the aliens now and had nothing else to do.

He watched Joel, bracing for a bad reaction. It was never easy to come out. Someone had told him it eventually got easier, but as far as Zac could tell that person had been lying.

After seven and a half tense seconds—Zac counted—Joel smiled. "Crowze and Grace, I would not have guessed *that*."

"Did you think I liked someone else?" Zac normally played his crushes close to his chest, and he wondered if he were giving out signs that he liked anyone. He didn't think he did. And he did *not* want to suddenly find himself with half a dozen crushes.

Joel shrugged. "There was no one I noticed. At first I thought you wanted Emily. But she and Oz..." He trailed off.

"Maybe for half a second," Zac confessed. But she and Oz were perfect together, and Emily was starting to feel like the sister he had never had. No romantic feelings there. "I'm usually only interested in one person at a time. And back on Earth things were different."

Joel's face darkened for a moment and the laugh he let out was bitter. "Oh, I know."

"I've seen people in three-way relationships. I don't know if that's something I want. But I am curious. At least when it comes to Grace and Crowze. What do you think?" A weight lifted off his shoulders as he confessed it. It didn't mean he had to act. But now he wasn't holding it tight inside. He could imagine himself pressed up tight against Grace with Crowze across from him, all three of them joined together in an intimate embrace. His body ached for it, for them. But was he ready? Did he *really* want it?

"The only way to know what they want would be to ask them." Why did Joel have to speak so much sense?

"Or I could not say anything, and I'll just be alone forever. That might be easier." Zac laughed as he said it, but he was only half joking. He would die of embarrassment if he said something and it turned out he had read into the situation incorrectly. Maybe that didn't make him all tough and strong and alpha, but he was getting a PhD in English literature, he wasn't a warrior or anything like that. And Crowze hadn't seemed to care. Neither had Grace. Zac searched for something, *anything*, to change the subject. "Since when do you have a beard?" he asked Joel, noting the light dusting of hair growing along his chin. "I thought we were beardless buddies." Zac had never quite managed to grow a beard of his own, not one that wasn't terribly patchy and rough. It didn't look good on him.

Joel held still for a moment and Zac wondered if he had said something wrong. The man was thinking, and it took him a few seconds. But after a moment he nodded to himself. "The Apsyns didn't care about giving me hormones. Apparently they didn't deem that *necessary* for my survival. Once I saw a doctor here, they got me on something appropriate. Even better than what I had back home. I'm starting to look more like myself."

Hormones? More like himself? The question must have shown on Zac's face.

"I'm trans," said Joel. "I haven't told many people. But the Zulir, the Synnrs at least, are accepting."

"Oh." He hadn't known that. Hadn't realized. But now that Zac thought about it, a few things made sense.

"Thank you for telling me." Was that the correct response? He hoped so. Joel was his friend. Beard or no. But before he could say anything more, Luci burst into the room.

"It's my birthday, congratulate me," she said as she flopped down onto Zac's bed, paying no attention to the several books he had laid out there.

"Happy birthday?" Zac said as he tried to save a few of the tomes. "How do you know?"

Luci shrugged, or tried to from her reclining position. "Well, we spent six months on Kilrym. And we've been here a month. And they had us on those space ships for like seventy years, or whatever. So that's a few birthdays. But I'm counting it as one. I'm nineteen now."

Zac laughed, but she had a point. "Happy birthday," he said again, more sure this time. He could forgive her for flopping down on the books... so long as none of the spines had cracked.

"You and Joel will have to figure out birthdays," she informed them. "We all will. This is our home now. We have to start thinking about these things."

That they did. And figuring out a birthday sounded easier than figuring out his heart.

Luci wasn't done with the news. "I'm planning a party. Do you think Crowze will let me use part of the estate?" she asked.

"You'll have to ask him," said Zac. He had spent enough time thinking about Crowze for today.

Luci's eyes got big and she leaned in close. "Or you could ask him for me," she said, doing the best puppy dog eyes he'd seen in a long time.

No. Not gonna happen. He hadn't talked to Crowze in four days, and he was happy to continue not talking to him until he figured out his own mind. "You're nineteen now," Zac said. "Doesn't that mean you have to plan your own events?"

Her eyes narrowed. "Fine." She rolled her eyes. "I guess I'll ask. I'm thinking of inviting everyone. The humans. Jori. The other Synnrs."

"What about Ax?" Zac asked. He thought he had seen an exchange between the two of them at Emily and Oz's bonding ceremony, but he wasn't sure.

"Jori and Ax?" Joel asked. "Maybe being involved with two people is going around."

Zac snapped his gaze to Joel and glared.

Luci made a sound of delight. "Who is it? Tell me, tell me." She bounced on the bed and Zac was caught between the acute betrayal from Joel and his concern for the books.

How was he getting out of this? It was one thing to tell Joel; Luci would have the information spread around the house in fifteen minutes. Thankfully, the alarm on his communicator went off. He checked the time. "Too bad, can't talk anymore. I have to go."

"No fair," Luci protested, grabbing his arm and tugging gently. "I want to know."

It didn't matter. Zac had a meeting with the queen.

***

It wasn't Zac's first trip to the palace, but he still marveled as he was led to Queen Serafina. Rich tapestries hung from the wall and artwork was on display in a mix of holographic and physical formats. Activity bustled around him. This wasn't a museum, it was a working government building. It still shocked him that he knew the queen.

She'd heard a report of him from one of her guards and had summoned him several weeks before. He'd been telling stories to children in the town square, half-remembered tales from Earth, and a few variations of his own. It wasn't like they would ever read the real Lord of the Rings. And if he had a few improvements, well, copyright didn't count in space.

Something about what he was doing had caught the queen's attention. And since then Zac had visited her a few times, telling stories from Earth and giving her his perspective on things. He never imagined that he would have the ear of a queen, and he didn't want to abuse the power. Not that he could. He was still just a human.

The queen hadn't been what he'd expected. There were no pearls or curly gray hair. She wasn't old. But she was fragile. Months before Zac had arrived on Aorsa, the queen had been severely injured in an attack that killed her consort and her Master of the Guard. It had left her weak.

She was recovering, but even with all of the most advanced medical technology it was a slow process. Scars danced up her arms, not hidden by a shawl or clothes or anything like that. She wanted people to see the angry red marks, to know that she had survived. She was tough, even if she looked like a strong wind could break her.

"Welcome, welcome. I'm so glad you could come," said Queen Serafina. She was reclining on a chair with a small teapot next to her, warm liquid steaming out of it.

Zac took his seat. Over the past few weeks this had become routine. As routine as a sit down with the queen could ever be. Simon, the Master of the Guard, barely spared him a glance. The queen's overprotective watchdog had become used to Zac's presence. Zac wasn't sure if he should be honored or a little bit insulted that the hulking barbarian of a man didn't see him as a threat.

And man he was. Simon was as human as Zac, though Zac didn't know if the man had been born among the Zulir or back on Earth. They had never got to chatting. Maybe one day he would be brave enough to ask. But not today.

"Thank you for having me, Your Majesty," said Zac. He gave a little bow and was rewarded with the tinkling laughter the queen gave him whenever he performed like an earthling. Bowing like that was not a Zulir custom. But she appreciated it.

"I couldn't leave you without the next part of the story," he said. The first time he'd arrived, he'd been more nervous than any first day of school or job interview, but now he felt comfortable enough to tease.

"Yes!" She clapped her hands together as Zac took his seat. "Where were we? The Peter boy was facing off against the horrible octopus doctor. Those arms..." She shuddered. "We do amazing things with prosthetics here," her eye quickly flicked down to her leg, and she continued as if she had not paused, "but nothing so monstrous. What comes next?"

Was he basically retelling Spider-Man 2? Possibly. Zac studied fiction, he didn't write it himself. Well, not unless you counted a bit of fanfiction, but that was neither here nor there. And it wasn't like the queen was ever going to meet Stan Lee. So he hoped that Marvel would forgive him.

He jumped into the story, using his whole body to tell it. His hands gesturing, leaning back and forward for emphasis, doing whatever it took to bring Peter Parker and his tales of bravery to life. But his heart wasn't in it.

It was still in that maze, caught between Crowze and Grace.

And the queen sensed it. "Leave Peter alone. I'm sure the boy will save himself another day. You seem preoccupied." She poured a cup of tea and slid it his way.

The only polite thing to do was to sit back down, though Zac had never been a particular lover of tea. But the Synnr drink was a bit different from what they had at home, sweeter, with a bit of fizz. He didn't hate it. "I'm sorry, Your Majesty." He had to get it together.

"I didn't ask for your apology, I want to know what's wrong." She raised an eyebrow, and he remembered that she was deadly at the negotiation table. She would need to be whenever this war got started.

He hated to think about it. It made his own issues pale in comparison. And he especially didn't want to complain about romance to the queen. Not when she had just lost her consort, not when she had to be worrying for her people. "I don't want to bother you with it," he said. "You have much more important things to deal with."

Something dangerous flashed across her face before she took another sip of tea and daintily set the cup down. "I think I know what I can deal with, Zac." A queenly rebuke. "What don't you want to bother me with?"

He wasn't getting out of this. Avoiding Luci was one thing, avoiding royalty? Yeah, not going to happen. "It's personal crap." *Crap*. He wasn't supposed to say crap in front of the queen. Shit. Oh no, he should definitely *not* say that.

"I live for personal... crap." She grinned, and he saw a hint of who she was when she wasn't recovering from near fatal injuries. She made the effort to say crap, rather than let her translator do the work for her. There seemed to be some kind of profanity filter on them; the translators didn't like to translate curse words.

He'd already come out to one person today. Wasn't that enough? He knew the queen wouldn't have an issue with his sexuality, but that didn't mean he wanted to talk about it. Was there such a thing as privacy on this damned planet? No. Not when he lived with half a dozen people, all of them in and out of each other's lives with nothing better to do.

Could he lie? No, lying to the queen was probably treason. And he did not want to be beheaded.

"Are you really sure you don't want to know what Doc Ock is about to do?" He scrambled to think of something interesting from the movie, but his mind went stubbornly blank. Suddenly he couldn't remember a thing.

"Yes," she said. "I would much rather know about the life of my friend then a fictional evil scientist." She paused. "But I do want to know about the fictional evil scientist. Later."

Yeah, he was going to have to make sure he remembered everything from that movie. It was probably worse than treason to leave the queen on a cliffhanger.

And she considered him a friend. That was nice. He needed as many of those as he could get. So he had to tell her. But maybe he could leave the names out of it. He doubted Grace or Crowze would be very happy about being brought to the queen's attention without their permission or knowledge.

"I—"

"Your Majesty." A woman carrying a digital tablet came in, her face pinched. "I apologize for my interruption, but the meeting you wanted scheduled is happening now. We were able to arrange it."

Meeting? Zac didn't ask. It wasn't his place. She might have considered him a friend, but that didn't mean he got to know the inner workings of queenly life. No doubt the queen had dozens of meetings to attend. And it meant he didn't have to say anything.

The queen looked annoyed. She pursed her lips and then carefully got up from her chair. It took time. Her muscles were still growing back and it looked like it hurt. Simon rushed forward to help her, but she held up a hand to stop him. "I am worthless if I cannot stand up from this simple chair."

"Our people do not follow you for your ability to stand, Your Majesty," Simon said, still getting closer. But the queen glared at him and he stopped.

What was going on there? He supposed if he wouldn't tell the queen about his personal life, she wasn't going to tell him about hers.

She finally stood, and though her cheeks were a bit flushed she was doing it on her own power. "It will be a couple of weeks before we can meet again. But I look forward to hearing both of your stories." She followed the woman out of the room without another word.

Yeah, Zac was afraid of that. But hopefully by the time a few weeks had passed, she would have forgotten it all.

Except for Doc Ock. He'd have to make that interesting.

Chapter Four

Grace was going crazy.

She couldn't stop thinking about Crowze or Zac, but she hadn't actually spoken to either of them in the two and a half weeks since the bonding ceremony. Maybe it was a bit immature, she didn't know. She didn't care.

There was a war on the horizon; she had bigger things to worry about than boys. At least that's what she said when she was awake. When she slept they were all she could think about, and she found herself waking with want and frustration.

It was supposed to be another day of training, another endless day of preparing for the war that would happen someday soon. Right now it was all posturing by armies and diplomats, and Grace was thankful she didn't have to play a part. Give her a weapon and point her in the right direction, that was all she needed. She didn't want to play along with silly political games. The Apsyns didn't think of her as a person; she would show them otherwise with blaster fire and violence.

But something felt off in the training facility.

Lena and Solan had disappeared two weeks before, sent off on some kind of training mission. They were bonded now, and Lena had her wings. But she and Solan hadn't been meshing as a unit, and they had been sent away for remedial training. Grace tried not to feel jealous, tried not to feel like she would be better than them, but she *would* be. She had spent her whole life wanting wings; she wouldn't squander the opportunity if it ever came.

What was so special about Lena that she found her Match only a month after arriving in Osais?

Thinking like that would drive Grace crazy.

She was in the middle of a meditation exercise when the door to her training room burst open and Crowze stuck his head in. Grace's heartbeat kicked up, and any of the peace and concentration from her meditation dissolved as she got a look at him. But today he was all business. Expression serious and looking at her like a fellow soldier, not a potential lover.

"Suit up, there's been an emergency. We have to go." He let the door fall closed behind him and didn't give her any more information. Grace didn't need more. She sprang to her feet and made her way to her locker where a uniform was waiting. Three minutes later, she was waiting in the front of the building with Crowze, Ax, Oz, Emily, and Jori. They clambered into a large vehicle and were off towards the center of the city.

"Lena and Solan uncovered disturbing information," Jori was telling them. Grace didn't know him very well, but he was a competent leader, and he had respected her when she had been a part of his team back on Kilrym. "We have reason to suspect that the Apsyns have planted a bomb somewhere in the center of the city. Our job will be to find it."

He handed out protective gear and they all put it on quietly. Grace caught a look that passed between Emily and Oz, something soft and intimate that didn't belong in this violent setting. She had to look away.

Anticipation hummed in her blood. She'd been training non-stop for weeks, secure in the knowledge that *something* was coming. And now it was here. Another woman might have been afraid of potentially being blown up.

Grace was relieved.

She didn't have a death wish, but she needed a purpose, and saving her people was good enough.

It only took a few minutes to get to the center of the city, and by the time they piled out of the van, Lena and Solan were already waiting. They split up into groups of two and somehow Grace ended up with Crowze. She wasn't going to argue. Not when there was a bomb somewhere in the city. She could work with him. It didn't mean they had to have pleasant conversation.

As they moved, she was surprised at how well they worked together. They didn't need to chat, and they communicated in a series of nods and hand gestures like they'd been doing this for years. It was comfortable, familiar. Unlike any other partnership she had.

But she wasn't going to dwell.

The main area of their quadrant was taken up by a school, and luckily today was not a school day. She and Crowze moved fast, but thoroughly, checking each of the rooms and clearing it of anything suspicious.

He worked well with her, not second-guessing, aware that she was a human and didn't have a spark, but adapting to that instead of thinking less of her. Whether Grace thought less of herself didn't matter right now.

They cleared the bottom level of the school and were heading up the stairs to the next. They could really use an entire team, but waiting for more people would take time that they didn't have.

Crowze finally broke their silence as they moved. "I wanted to—"

"Keep to the job," Grace told him. They weren't having a conversation now. They weren't having a conversation *ever* if she could manage that. Some might have said that repressing emotions wasn't a healthy response, but Grace had to do what she had to do.

"After this, I'd like to talk," he pressed on. She hated how good he looked in his uniform. It covered up most of his body, just letting her see his eyes and a bit of his face. But he filled it out well, too well.

After this, Grace wanted a lot of things. It didn't mean she would get them.

"Check the east hallway, I'll take the west." She took off before he had a chance to object. They met back at the staircase after a few minutes, each of the rooms on this floor empty as well. There was only one more floor, and they cleared that in no time. But the staircase had a window, and it gave them a good vantage point of the central city.

Grace lifted the glass and leaned out, trying to get a better look. She could feel the steady presence of Crowze's body behind her, and it was distracting. She wanted to lean back and feel him, and she wanted to kick herself for even considering it.

Was she going crazy?

Crazy with lust, maybe. She needed to get laid. To get the desire out of her system. Maybe a night with Crowze would do it. Or a night with Crowze and Zac. She could imagine it, hard masculine bodies all around her, lips pressed against her, limbs entangled. It would be overwhelming, decadent. But would it be enough?

Her grip slipped and she pitched forward, almost through the window. Before she could readjust, Crowze's strong arm wrapped around her chest and pulled her back. "I've got you," he said, voice gruff and close.

Grace tore away from him, careful to move to the side to avoid falling. "I'm human, not fragile," she spat. "I don't need your protection."

Crowze's eyebrows scrunched together and he looked confused, as confused as a man in full defensive gear *could* look. "Did you want to fall out the window?"

"I wasn't going to fall." She wasn't. And a tiny part of her would rather fall then need to be protected. "There's nothing here. Let's go back." Out of the school and away from any temptation. Or open windows.

Crowze looked like he was about to say something, but he snapped his mouth shut and they headed back to meet up with the others. Hopefully one of them had found and disarmed the bomb.

It didn't take long for Solan and Lena to join them. No explosive. No more clues. No idea where the deadly device was lurking, ready to deal destruction.

Frustration mounted. Grace knew she was getting snippy and she could feel the tension in the air. They were ready to snap.

But Lena broke through it all, looking up at the palace that loomed over them. "The queen," she said. "They want to take out the queen."

***

Crowze had to focus or people were going to die.

And with Grace running alongside him, she was in danger, too. He would stab himself in the heart before he let harm come to her by any mistake of his own, but harm could come anyway if they didn't find this bomb. He didn't waste time wishing she could stay back, could let him rush into danger in her place. She was as much a warrior as he was, and he wouldn't ever say otherwise.

"Do we get her out of the palace?" asked Grace as they made their way through the gate.

"Don't be foolish, that only makes her more vulnerable." Crowze knew it was unnecessarily harsh, but he couldn't pull the words back. What had gotten into him?

Grace glared at him, then turned to Solan. "What's our next move?"

Solan took a minute to think, and Crowze wanted to shake him, to force him to hurry. It was no use, and after a moment Solan spoke. "There's no point in hitting the palace if they can't hit the queen. If there is a bomb, it will be near her quarters."

"Wait," Lena said, holding up a hand. "They could also be trying to cause chaos. If they couldn't get a bomb into her quarters, they could still set one off and use the confusion to kill or abduct her. We need eyes on the queen. And the guards need to be ready in case we've got more Apsyns coming."

She had a point. "The Master of her Guard will be with her. Let's go."

They rushed into the palace and were shepherded through by a fretting servant.

When Lena suggested the bomb was in the palace, Crowze had thought she was crazy. How would someone even get a bomb into a building as protected as this one? But they moved with haste, and Crowze spotted several points of entry he could use if he had sinister intentions.

They were up several more flights of stairs and down two corridors before they made it to Queen Serafina's private chambers. Crowze had never been here before. His family might've been aristocratic, but they did not travel in royal circles. Too political, too complicated.

There was no use in getting caught up in Synnr politics, and he couldn't imagine anyone who would want to.

His mind stuttered when he saw Zac sitting beside the queen. Their heads were close together, as if they were sharing secrets, and from the smile that slid off the queen's face when she saw them, she and Zac had grown quite close. When had that happened?

How had that happened?

Zac was keeping secrets. Crowze wanted to know them all.

Zac sprung to his feet when they entered. "What are you doing here?" He was staring straight at Crowze before he tore his gaze away to look at Grace.

"What are *you* doing here?" Grace shot back.

"Your highness," Solan addressed the queen. "We have reason to believe there's been a bomb planted in the palace. Where is your Master of the Guard?"

The queen studied Solan for several moments, taking his measure. He must have lived up to her standard. "Simon, come in," she finally said. "Your presence has been requested." Another human came out from a side room, his hand on his blaster, eyes intent. This was Simon, the queen's Master of the Guard. Crowze had heard of him. Not many humans rose so high in the ranks so swiftly. But from the protectiveness radiating from the man, he took his job seriously.

"We have evidence that Apsyns have planted a bomb somewhere in the center of the city. We believe it is inside the palace. And we believe it could be a distraction. We need your guards on the lookout, both searching for the bomb and prepared for a secondary attack. Can you do that?" Solan quickly broke down the threat, and Crowze wanted to move. They were wasting precious minutes.

Simon studied him silently before nodding. He pulled out a communication tablet and typed something into it. "You two," he nodded to Grace and Crowze, "stay with the queen and her guest. You," this was to Lena and Solan, "you have clearance to search the queen's quarters. The rest of the guards will be on the lookout. Move."

They moved.

"And what if this is a trap?" asked Simon. Solan and Lena were already gone, but the thought seemed to have just occurred to him. "What if false information has been laid and someone is coming for her majesty?"

"We need be on high alert," said Grace. "Your guards let us right in. If there is a turncoat..."

Crowze didn't want to think it, but how else would someone get a bomb into the palace?

Taking the queen outside seemed dangerous, but would it be worse than staying in?

Zac was standing now, but he hadn't said anything. His eyes kept darting between Crowze and Grace and then back to the queen. Was something going on there? How exactly had Zac gotten into the queen's good graces? And how far into those graces was he? Crowze knew he had other things to worry about, but it mattered to him. He could focus on two *punting* things at once.

"If someone doesn't say something, we won't need a bomb to explode. The tension will be enough to decimate us all." Queen Serafina grinned as she looked at them. She didn't look scared of the bomb threat. But she had lived her entire life bouncing from one threat to another. It hadn't been long since her husband had been stolen from her in another attack. She had to be resilient or she would break.

"Your Majesty..." said Zac, tone caught between warning and respectful.

Her eyes got big and her grin grew. "Oh! You never told me what was bothering you the last time we spoke. I'm sensing something."

It didn't take a psychic to sense something like this. And this was Crowze's moment. He had Grace and Zac in front of him, and they couldn't leave, not until it was safe. He had to take a shot. He hadn't exactly wanted to do this in front of the queen, but he had no other choice.

It was completely inappropriate. Unprofessional. But sometimes it was the only chance a person got. If he didn't say something now, he couldn't be sure that he'd ever get the chance again.

Besides, they might all get blown up. He didn't want to die regretting that he hadn't taken a chance.

"I'm sorry." He looked quickly at Grace as he spoke. She scowled, but didn't tell him to shut up this time. The queen made a little noise of excitement and he was sure that if things were slightly less perilous, she would have sat back in her chair and watched the drama unfold with glee. Crowze had to ignore her, as much as one could ignore a queen when standing in her chamber. "I went about this all wrong," Crowze continued.

Zac remained silent, but he was watching Crowze, eyes full of curiosity.

"I did not mean to cause you pain," he said to Grace. Zac furrowed his brow, and Crowze realized that Zac didn't know everything that had happened on the night of the bonding ceremony. "I kissed Grace before I kissed you," Crowze explained. It sounded terrible when he said it like that. He couldn't encapsulate the emotions that he'd been feeling, the desire, and excitement, and trepidation at finally making his move.

The queen let out a little hum and then cleared her throat. Zac did his best to ignore it.

"I approached you both because I want you both. Together. I was playing no games." This he addressed mostly to Grace. He had suffered her ire for the past weeks and he suspected that it was because of what she'd seen. Zac had mostly stayed away. And Crowze wanted to change that.

So why was Zac still silent?

"We're human. Both of us," Grace pointed out, as if Crowze didn't know that. As if he cared.

"Yes, I'm very aware of that," said Crowze. It wasn't the first time Grace had pointed it out, and he didn't understand why. Plenty of humans lived among the Zulir. A woman like Grace was just as much of a Synnr as he was.

Why did she think it mattered to him? He wanted her for the fire he could see burning inside her, her passion, her strength, her drive, and her beauty. Did she think it mattered to him where her ancestors had come from? Where her mother had come from?

He was confessing everything else, but those thoughts were private, thoughts he just wanted to give to Grace and Zac. The queen didn't need to hear it.

But why wasn't Zac speaking up?

Crowze turned to him, ready to say something, but Simon's communicator buzzed. He said something into it and then interrupted.

"As fascinating as all of this is, we have work to do. They found the bomb. We need to get her majesty out of here."

Everything moved fast after that. Simon, Crowze, and Grace shepherded the queen out of her quarters, meeting up with trusted guards to get her out of a secret entrance and to a secure location.

Crowze wanted to go back for Zac, but at the moment security protocols dictated that he stay with the queen. He knew it was the right move tactically, but that didn't mean that his heart accepted it. And by the time everything was over, by the time the bomb had been defused, and the queen returned safely to her chambers, Zac was long gone.

Crowze and Grace were pulled into separate debriefing sessions, and at the end of the night Crowze was left alone. Again.

Chapter Five

Zac dreamt of explosions. And he had never been more grateful that the sun didn't set on Aorsa at this time of year. When he woke up on the edge of screaming at two AM he could roll out of bed and look at the bright sky and pretend everything was all right. It had been a few days since the bomb was discovered in the palace.

A few days since Crowze had dropped a bombshell of his own.

It was what Zac wanted. The secret desire he had barely been able to tell Joel. The thing he was still trying to wrap his mind around. Was he ready for a relationship like that?

He didn't know if it mattered. Grace and Crowze had disappeared in the flurry of activity and Zac hadn't seen either of them since. It was quite the feat considering he lived on Crowze's property.

Was Zac supposed to make a move now?

He regretted not saying anything back in the queen's quarters, but he had been in a state of shock, between Crowze's confession and the impending threat of being blown to pieces. He wasn't a soldier. His life had never involved dealing with danger, not unless you counted mold spores from old books or the occasional paper cut.

And when he thought about that, he wondered what Crowze or Grace could possibly see in him. Crowze and Grace together he understood. They were both Synnrs, both warriors. Why did they need a bookish earthling with a penchant for telling stories? He'd never even been in a fight.

The only way to know would be to ask, but Zac hadn't got up the courage to do it yet.

Hopefully today he wouldn't need to. Lena was finally back from wherever she had been sent, and he, Joel, Luci, Emily, and another human named Gayle were having lunch together. The Zulir food was great, the flavors sometimes familiar enough to make him homesick, but usually with enough of a twist to remind him that he was eating alien food on an alien planet. They were all shunted off to the back room of the restaurant they were eating in, and Lena was talking animatedly with Luci, both of them planning the younger woman's birthday party.

Lena looked good, healthy, and happier than he'd ever seen her. Matching with Solan suited her well. She had wanted a warrior's life, wanted to stake her place in the Synnr military, and now she had. And along with it she had found love in her Match. That was two humans down. Zac couldn't help but see a pattern. Who would be next?

"Between getting punched in the head a dozen times and listening to Luci plan her birthday party, I know what I prefer," Gayle leaned in and whispered conspiratorially. He remembered her saying something about being a boxer in her old life, so when she said punched she meant it.

Zac felt a bit disloyal for laughing. But the party was all that Luci had been talking about since she'd announced it.

"So we're definitely inviting Jori and the rest of them," said Luci, inflecting enough on Jori's name to make it clear she needed him to be there.

"Obviously Solan is going to be your date, and Emily you're bringing Oz. I expect presents. It's not every day that a girl turns nineteen."

"Yeah, and we still don't know if you did turn nineteen," Lena teased.

Luci rolled her eyes. "What? Am I not supposed to have a birthday ever again?"

"I think Lena has a point," said Joel, nodding along. "Do we get to pick the age, too?" he asked. "Because I'm happy to stay forty-five forever."

"You're forty-five?" Luci asked, then her eyes got big and she slammed her lips together.

Joel laughed. "I'll take that as the compliment you meant. Right?" He stared at her with a grin.

Luci nodded quickly.

"Jori said he could cater the event," Luci said, turning back to the plans and away from age-related blunders. "Or, well, I guess he could have it catered. I don't think he plans to cook everything. But that's one thing that we don't have to worry about. Zac, did you ask Crowze if we could use the estate?"

"Yeah, Zac, did you ask Crowze? Joel asked. His eyes sparkled with mischief. But as far as Zac knew Joel hadn't shared his secret with anyone.

Luci suspected. She had to. Lena had been gone and couldn't have seen anything happen. Zac didn't know about the others. If something was going to happen he would have to get used to their curiosity. The Synnrs might not have cared about the makeup of relationship groups, but the humans would.

Would they still accept Zac if he were with both Crowze and Grace?

Joel didn't seem to have a problem with it. He hoped the rest of them would be cool.

Was that it then? Had he decided to try? If Crowze actually came to him and asked him and Grace out, would he accept? Did he want to go find them and make the first, or rather the second, move? No, he wasn't there yet. But if Crowze and Grace approached him, he wanted to see where it would go.

"Earth to Zac," Luci prompted.

"Earth?" Gayle asked. She tilted her head and the scar tracing the side of her face was illuminated in the light. Zac didn't know how she'd gotten it, whether it had come from her boxing career. She hadn't shared and he didn't know her well enough to deserve an explanation.

Luci rolled her eyes. "Fine, *Aorsa* to Zac. Have you talked to Crowze?"

"I told you to talk to him," he shot back. "You're an adult now."

"Uh, I was an adult last year, too. And my mom still called and made my doctor's appointments." Luci crossed her arms, gaze set in challenge.

"That doesn't make you sound like a grown-up," Emily pointed out.

"Shit!" said Lena, jolting in her chair and grabbing her communicator from where it sat on the table. "I've got to head back. Training session."

"Wait!" Luci said, reaching out to grab her arm and keep her from getting away. "Can we see them?"

"What?" Lena asked.

"Your wings," Luci prompted. "Can we see your wings?"

Lena grinned, eyes lit up in excitement. She took a deep breath and electricity crackled in the room. Then they were there, blue and green and red, all lit up and flaring out around them. Zac wanted to touch, but he figured that was probably both rude and dangerous. Would it be like touching a live wire? He wasn't about to find out.

Lena let them admire for a minute before pulling her wings back. "I really do have to go."

"I'll walk you," Zac offered. If they were going to spend the next hour party planning, he was glad for the escape. Gayle smacked him gently on the thigh as he got up and he turned to make sure he was facing just her and stuck his tongue out. She could've offered to walk with Lena, but she hadn't thought of it fast enough.

They left the restaurant and headed up the street. The training facility was only two blocks away, and from there Zac could catch a tram or a taxi to get back home.

"You're coming to Solan's brother's wedding, right?" Lena asked as they crossed a street and almost got hit by a speeding bike.

Zac made a rude gesture at the biker, who was long gone, before turning back to Lena. "I am?" He couldn't remember hearing anything about it, but it had been a busy few days.

"You are," Lena said in a tone that told him he did *not* have another option.

"I guess I am. When is it?" He felt like he was bouncing from one party to another. The bonding ceremony, Luci's birthday, now this wedding.

"Next week. I'll make sure you guys have all the information. His brother seems nice. And so does his husband to be. And besides, we could all use more friends."

They definitely could. And it was heartening to hear that Lena was accepting of Solan's brother. Maybe Zac didn't have anything to worry about.

Lena left him to rush up the stairs and get ready for her training session, and just as the door was about to close behind her it burst open again and Grace rushed out. She froze when she saw Zac standing there. Only a dozen feet separated them, but it might as well have been an ocean. He thought Grace was going to turn away. He would bet his life savings on it. But she took a deep breath and stepped toward him. Good thing he didn't actual *have* a life savings anymore.

"What are you doing here?" It wasn't an accusation. Just curiosity. Grace looked good. Energetic. Not at all like someone who'd searched for a bomb and almost gotten blown up.

Still, Zac's eyes searched over her, looking for any evidence of hurts. He knew it was illogical, knew exactly what had happened, but he couldn't stop himself. He was happy to see she was fine. More than fine.

"Lena had lunch with a few of us. I walked her back. Heading back now." There was a train station one street over and it would take him close to home. His mind was spinning with the things Crowze had said, what he had suggested. Grace wasn't giving him so much as a hint to what she wanted, but what did that mean? Of course, they were out in the open, standing on the steps of her workplace. Of course she'd be professional.

"To Crowze's estate." It wasn't a question. Zac couldn't quite read her expression. Was she upset about that? Upset that he lived near Crowze? Or was it something else?

"Yeah, you've been to the house." Now would be the perfect time to say *something*. But Zac's words were caught in his throat. He wanted to ask her what she thought, if she was interested in kissing him again. But he couldn't.

"I have to..." Grace nodded down the street in the opposite direction of where Zac was headed; she took one step but didn't move any further.

"Of course. It was good to see you." And out of habit he leaned in for a goodbye hug. His arms were around Grace before he could think better of it. She was stiff for a moment before she relaxed, her body an alluring mix of strength and softness that he knew he could get lost in. But in a blink the hug was over and she stepped back.

"I've got to go." And then she was off.

Zac took a step and almost followed after her before he thought better of it. He needed to be sure. He had a feeling that once he started down a new path there would be no turning back

***

More training.

Grace didn't know that she could get sick of training. It had been the staple of her life for years. Keeping her muscles in shape, her reflexes fresh. She had to be on alert every second for some kind of danger.

She was on alert. Everyone was. But how long did it take for a war to start? The Apsyns were up to something. They were *always* up to something.

Maybe it would be better if the Synnrs just attacked. Get this whole thing over with.

Maybe that was why Grace wasn't in charge. She would just command all of the ships in the armada to fire on Apsyn facilities until their army was dust. And then she would be promptly tried for war crimes. Okay, not the best idea.

So training it was. And today she was working with Emily. Grace was making an effort to get to know the humans around her better. She had given the humans rescued from Kilrym a few pointers about life among the Synnrs, but until recently she had tended to avoid the ones that she worked with. As if hanging out with them would remind all of the Zulir around them that Grace was human. As if they couldn't tell.

But was it a problem that just existed in her own head?

Her mind had been caught on what Crowze said in the queen's quarters. *Everything* he had said. But mostly his confusion when she reminded him that she was human. He hadn't cared. Not in a way that said it wasn't important or that he didn't respect her lineage. But he saw her for who she was and the fact that she didn't have wings didn't matter.

Emily's elbow caught her across the jaw and Grace had to get her head back in the game.

Distraction would get her killed. And she was plenty distracted these days.

She hit back just as hard, feeling a deep sense of satisfaction when Emily grunted against a punch to her stomach. She had improved a lot in the past month and a half. When she showed up she had no experience fighting. She was plenty spry, with a history of acrobatics and gymnastics, but she had never thrown a punch.

Now she could reliably land a few blows every time she and Grace sparred. And once she got full control of her spark, Grace wouldn't stand a chance against her.

Nothing was stopping her from using it now, but Emily tended to get laser focused and forgot that she could access her powers at any time. Grace wasn't about to remind her. She had been shocked by a spark before and it wasn't pleasant.

The timer buzzed, calling an end to their sparring session. Emily jumped back and was all smiles while it took Grace a minute to shift out of the fighting headspace. They walked to the side of the mat and grabbed their own towels to wipe off their sweat while rehydrating.

"You're getting better," Grace said. "But something's still holding you back." Grace was just a sparring partner, not Emily's trainer, but it didn't mean she couldn't give her pointers now that they were off the mat. After all, Grace had been part of the Synnr military for almost a decade.

Emily blew out a tired breath before gulping down more of her water. When she was done, she sighed. "I thought I did pretty good," she said. "I got you in the face. I think you're going to have a hell of a bruise on your jaw." She was half smile, half grimace. As if she were proud and ashamed at the same time.

"I was distracted." Grace regretted saying it as soon as the words came out. These humans didn't leave things alone. If she said she was distracted, they'd want to know why.

"Distracted?" Emily asked, right on cue.

"It's nothing." And Grace hoped Emily would let it lie. *We're not friends, we don't need to talk.* Yeah, that didn't work. Emily seemed to want to be friends with everyone, even Grace, and every time they sparred she tried to use these little breaks to get closer to her. This was the first time Grace was really letting it happen.

But she needed friends. That had become abundantly clear, though maybe not *this* friend.

"Come on," Emily cajoled. "What's got you distracted? Think of it like a training thing. Maybe if I can distract you again I'll actually be able to pin you."

That surprised a laugh out of Grace. "That's not happening. And what would Oz say about that?"

"Huh? Oh!" Emily's pale cheeks flamed. "I thought you were into dudes," she said.

Earthlings. They made things way too complicated.

"I am. I'm into anybody who catches my eye." Crowze. Zac. She had two eyes. She saw two guys. More than enough for her. Maybe too much. Was she ready to take a chance?

"That's..." Emily took another big drink of her water and let the thought hang there.

Grace didn't let it get to her. What was the point? If humans from Earth were going to be so judgmental she didn't need them. Though she wasn't sure if Emily was judging her right now or if she was just nervous. It didn't matter. The buzzer timed, signaling that their break was over.

They went back to the mat and Grace took control of the sparring match from the start. She wasn't going to let Emily get her, and she wasn't going to be distracted by the feelings that kept churning inside of her. Emily didn't have a chance to land a blow. Grace's jaw tingled and she did not want more bruises.

She wrestled Emily down to the ground and had her pinned, holding one arm in a stress position that could easily break it if she applied just a bit more pressure.

But this time it wasn't Emily who forgot about her spark. It was Grace. Her only warning was a slight crackle in the air before Emily lashed out, her wings flashing as she sent a jolt of spark at Grace, the power strong enough to blow Grace back and off of Emily.

Grace tried to get up. She did. She rolled on her side, but her vision was blurry and she was a bit disoriented. She could barely move. Emily managed to get a hold of her and hit her lightly in several spots, indicating kill shots. The buzzer cut off the match, declaring Emily the victor.

Grace slumped down, laying on the sparring mat. Emily stood over her and offered a hand up, but Grace turned her head away. Stupid. Sloppy.

She needed wings of her own.

As soon as she was done training for the day, Grace was going to check the Matching database again. She didn't have time for romance, not when she needed the power a Match could give her.

Chapter Six

Aunt Margo kept looking out the window. She was one of his favorite relatives, a human woman only about ten years older than himself, and Matched to his uncles Ryden and Ginn for nearly twenty years. Ryden was his mother's youngest brother and he had always treated Crowze like more of a brother than an annoying nephew. And Crowze knew he had earned the title of annoyance once or twice.

"What are you looking for?" Crowze asked. It was distracting, the way she kept looking. They were in one of the receiving rooms at his estate. There was nothing interesting to see other than some trees and the occasional bird flying by.

"Doesn't one of your humans live in the house down the way?" Margo asked. "Not Romy's girl, the other one."

Romy was Grace's father and a close friend of Ginn. Of course they all knew who Grace was. Margo was asking about Zac.

Crowze hadn't told them much. His uncles and aunt didn't live on the estate, unlike most of the rest of his family. It meant he only got to see them once or twice a month, whenever they made the effort to come out or he went into the city to see them. They claimed they needed the privacy, but Crowze missed them, even if all three of them had never lived on the estate together. Uncle Ryden had moved out when he found Margo and Ginn.

But he wouldn't let himself be upset today. They were here, and he was going to enjoy it while it lasted. "He's not there," said Crowze. "I think he had to go to the city." Crowze wasn't keeping tabs on Zac, but he had noticed a taxi earlier in the day and he had seen Zac get into it. Was he meeting with the queen again? He didn't mention that part to Margo. She was fascinated enough as it was.

"So things are moving along?" Ryden asked. It had only been natural to ask his uncles and aunt about how to go about wooing two people, and now they were invested in Crowze's relationship. Crowze was pretty sure each one of them wanted to take over and force him to do exactly as they said. He was moving far too slowly for their liking, but Crowze moved at his own pace.

"They know I'm interested." And so did the queen. And her hulking guard. Hopefully those two had forgotten that by now.

"They know you're interested and...?" Ginn asked. He looked at Crowze like he expected him to make some sort of revelation.

What was Crowze supposed to say? "I told them I wanted both of them."

"And?" asked Margo.

And, and, and. What was he supposed to say?

"*And* they're thinking," said Crowze. He hoped they were thinking. If he had been the kind to pray he would've prayed they were thinking.

He'd seen Zac a few times, though they hadn't done more than exchange a pleasant hello. He hadn't seen Grace. He didn't know if she was avoiding him or if they were just being pulled in opposite training directions. He hoped she wasn't ignoring him.

He was getting tired of hoping.

Ginn made a sound of disgust. "You *think*? They're thinking? You need to make a move if you want anything to happen, boy. How do you think anyone finds a Match?" He shot a heated look towards Ryden and then reached for Margo's hand and kissed her fingers.

Crowze wanted what they had.

He could imagine Grace and Zac sitting right in here with him having some sort of inconsequential conversation, a silly argument that they kept going for too long just to have a reason to make up once it was done. He could imagine sparring with Grace and talking philosophy with Zac. He imagined Zac would have a lot to say on the subject.

So how did he get them to the next step? It was even more complicated with Zac living on the property. Some might've thought it made things easier, but Crowze was caught in an ethical dilemma. He didn't want Zac or any of the humans to think their home was contingent on keeping him happy, or engaging in a relationship with him.

He wanted Zac's heart and his body freely given. The same with Grace. Crowze ended up saying some of that and Ryden gave him an indulgent smile.

"You have a soft heart," he said.

"I'm a warrior." Crowze had to defend himself. He left battlefields covered in blood with wounds a man shouldn't survive. He still had nightmares sometimes of the things he had to do.

Softhearted? No.

"It was no insult," said Ryden. "You may be a soldier, but you're also a good man. And you're always there to help. Anyone would be lucky to have you as a Match and a partner."

A Match. Crowze didn't think about it most days. But seeing two of his friends so happily Matched in close succession made him wonder. He had never bothered to submit his information to the Matching Bureau; he had no need for some database somewhere to hold that information for him.

But what would it be like to be connected to someone, or two someones, on that level?

"Get your head out of your ass, kid," said Ginn. "Go get those humans. I want to meet them."

Ginn was right. The time for waiting was over. If Grace and Zac weren't coming to him, he would go to them. He wasn't giving up until all hope was lost.

***

It was a bit surreal to be back in Queen Serafina's quarters as if nothing had happened. The only sign of the bomb threat from a few days ago was an increased security presence. The queen smiled and greeted him just as she had every other day when he had come to see her.

Was her smile a bit more strained around her eyes? Possibly. But Zac figured a queen was under a lot of stress all the time. It was bound to show eventually.

"I'm so glad you could make it," said the queen. "I hope it wasn't too dreadful to get past the brutes outside." She glared at the door and then swung her head around to look towards a second door that led into the small office that Simon used as his headquarters.

Zac wanted to ask what that look was about. Of course he was dying of curiosity, but he kept that to himself. He had noticed glances between the queen and her guard more than once, but he didn't want to upset her by saying that he had an idea of what was going on between them. Or what could be going on between them.

Besides, it hadn't been very long since her husband died. He didn't know if the queen wanted to risk her heart again. Of course, she was a queen, and she had responsibilities of her own. Her heart would have nothing to do with any sort of marriage she entered into.

"No trouble getting in," Zac assured her. One of the guards had nearly gotten to third base when he patted Zac down for any weapons, but Zac kept that to himself. It wasn't an appropriate comment to make to the queen, and she wouldn't understand the reference anyway. He hadn't yet familiarized himself with sports that the Synnrs played, but he was pretty sure they didn't have baseball. Maybe the humans could introduce it to them.

"I wanted you to come back sooner, but you know how these things get," she said. Zac didn't know, but he kept quiet. "I swear they would wrap me in protective cloth and throw me in the vault if they could. I don't need protection. Or not any more than any other queen needs."

She was still as fragile as she ever was, but Zac could see the steel in her spine. She was determined to heal and lead her people just as she had before. She wouldn't let something like a bomb threat stop her.

"Have there been any other issues?" Zac asked, switching the question he meant to ask at the last moment. He almost asked if she was doing okay, but he was sure she didn't want to answer that.

The queen laughed. "I'm dealing with the normal trauma, but it's not the first time someone's tried to blow me up, and it takes much more than that to kill me." She got quiet for a moment and looked skyward, as if she forgot Zac was in the room. "If only that were true for those closest to me," she said like an afterthought, almost too quiet for Zac to hear.

It was private, a hidden depth of her emotion, of her grief for her husband and her former Master of the Guard. Those weren't the only people she had lost. Zac knew enough about her history to know that the royal family was riddled with untimely deaths. He supposed that's what happened when people ruled in the middle of a war.

And it made Zac think about loss.

He'd been so caught up in figuring out what his attraction to two people meant that he hadn't considered that they were both soldiers in a military perched on the edge of war. They could fly off one day and never come back.

Would his heart survive if he fell in love with two people and then lost them both?

From the way his stomach dropped, he didn't want to consider it. He didn't want to think about Grace's eyes closed for the last time, her chest still, heart no longer beating. He didn't want to think about Crowze buried deep in the ground, or burned to ash, whatever Zulir did with their dead. He didn't want to think about it. But he had to.

Was love worth the risk?

And when had he started thinking of them in terms of love? Zac was ready to take his usual seat and start telling stories. He was ready to get back to normal. He had done his best to remember Spider-Man and he was pretty sure he could do the story justice. He'd been practicing his web slinging and wished he could jump from rooftop to rooftop to truly sell the character. But a good storyteller could weave the images with words alone.

Before he took a seat, the queen stopped him. "I'm afraid I don't have time for stories today." She said it regretfully.

"Oh?" Then what was Zac doing here? She had specifically requested his presence. But what use did he have if he wasn't telling her stories from Earth?

"Go ahead and sit," the queen commanded. She sat across the table from him, but unlike the normal smiling face he saw when he told her stories, today she was serious. "We have a chance to stop this war before it starts. The Apsyns want to meet. They want a summit between me and their prince. I don't know what they'll offer us, and I don't know what we'll need to concede. But we might be able to stop the bloodshed. And if I can protect thousands of lives, I'll do it."

Zac didn't know a summit was possible. From everything he'd been told about the relationship between the Synnrs and Apsyns, there was no stopping this war. They hated each other beyond reason.

And the Apsyns seemed evil. They believed their species, the Zulir, was superior to all others in the galaxy. It was only the fact that they didn't yet have a fleet of conquering spaceships that had kept them from leaving to colonize the galaxy. They probably had plenty of justifications for why that was, but Zac didn't need to hear them. He had heard enough people spewing that kind of hate back on Earth. He didn't buy it then and he didn't buy it now.

But he also could have been biased against the Apsyns. After all, they had held him and his friends as prisoners for months performing medical experiments on them and forcing them to perform as entertainment to further fund the experimentation.

"I wish you luck," Zac said. He might not like the Apsyns, but stopping a war seemed good.

"I'm not sure it's possible," the queen admitted. "But I hope. And I'm telling you this for a reason. I making you a special advisor and I want you to come with me. According to the terms both the prince and I can bring a specific set of advisors and guards. We're going to a neutral location. It's as safe as we can make it. I've appreciated our time together and I think you'll bring a unique perspective to things."

A unique perspective? Zac was just a student from Earth. He was no one special. It was pure chance that he had grabbed the attention of the queen. But maybe that was what counted.

"And I'm human," Zac realized. "The Apsyns don't like us."

The queen smiled mischievously. "No, they don't."

Zac didn't want to be a pawn. He didn't want to be a pet human on display, there only to annoy the enemy. But the queen was giving him an order. And a promotion. How could he say no? Besides, this was a once-in-a-lifetime opportunity. He would've never gotten to stop the war back home.

Back on Earth. He had to stop thinking about his home. Aorsa was his home now.

"I can't wait," said Zac with a bit of false sincerity.

The queen smiled, this time genuine. "Wonderful," she said, clapping her hands together. "You will need to undergo a few medical tests before you go to the space station where we're having the summit. It's all routine, I promise, and confidential. And we have to have this expedited."

"Medical tests?" Zac didn't like the sound of that. After six months in Apsyn custody, he would be happy to never undergo a medical test again.

"It's all routine," the queen assured him. "Nothing to worry about. The appointment has already been made for you at a clinic downtown. It should only take an hour or so. The summit will be on a space station, and we have to ensure that everyone is completely healthy. We wouldn't want to accidentally spread a contagious disease."

He supposed she had a point. And, again, he couldn't resist an order from the queen. So he left.

Medical tests. Fucking great.

Chapter Seven

Crowze found Zac wandering the path behind his house, looking like his mind was on another planet. Maybe it was. Maybe he was consumed with thoughts of his homeland. Crowze had been so obsessed with wanting him that he hadn't stopped to consider that.

Did that make him selfish?

He hoped not, though he knew a bit of selfishness went into his position as aristocrat and head of his family. But he didn't want to be selfish today. He wanted Zac.

"Hello," he greeted.

Zac jolted and came to a halt. He held up the book he was holding as if it could ward off an attack, but relaxed when he saw it was Crowze. "Oh. Hello."

If Crowze wanted things to work out he needed to actually spend time with Zac and Grace. And now he had at least half an opportunity. "You look like you could use a friend. Or a seat."

Zac glanced over at the bench and he looked intently, as if he was doing some complex math in his brain. Then his cheeks turned red and Crowze had an idea of what he was thinking about.

"I promise to be on my best behavior." He held up his hands as if it would be evidence enough.

"Is that what you think I want?" Zac asked as he took a seat.

Crowze sat down beside him, careful to leave just a hint of space between them. If he pushed, Zac might go away. Crowze didn't want that. He wanted Zac and Grace sitting beside him, enjoying the pleasant afternoon sun. He wanted more than that, but he couldn't have everything all at once.

Crowze knew what he wanted. Zac knew what he wanted. And the fact that Zac was here right now suggested that maybe he wanted the same thing.

Or maybe he just needed a friend. Crowze could be that friend. For now.

But Zac leaned in close and Crowze smelled Zac's soap. It was the same kind Crowze used. His servants stocked the human house with the same products that were in his own home and he liked that this was something that he and Zac shared. But there was also an underlying scent that was just *him*, something that mixed with their shared soap and made it uniquely his.

Crowze stretched his arm and let it fall along the back of the bench they were sitting on. He didn't quite touch Zac, but it was a close thing. And it gave Zac room to lean closer into him, which he did.

"Would you like something to drink? I should've offered earlier." Crowze didn't know where his manners had gone. But he could call for a servant to bring them something at any moment.

"No, I'm fine," said Zac. He stared out into the manicured lawn and the wildflowers beyond it. And then he sighed. "Do you think there's anything that could stop this war?" Zac asked.

This was a heavy subject. No wonder Zac had looked far away. "I'm not sure," said Crowze. Honestly, he didn't think so. The Apsyns seemed ready for a fight. But it had been a long time since they'd engaged in a full-blown war.

"I get that the Apsyns are dicks, but why are things so strained? What started it?" Zac asked. He flexed his fingers before curling them into fists and letting them rest on top of his legs.

Crowze wanted to reach over and lace their fingers together, but he didn't want Zac to retreat. So he let him stay where he was. It was all ancient history to Crowze. Something he had known since he was just a boy. All Synnrs knew it. And he assumed the Apsyns had their own version of events.

"It started a long, long time ago. Back when the first aliens made contact with us." Crowze reached deep into his memory to recall the story. "They weren't like us. Or like humans. The Apsyns saw their differences as inferiority, even if they had such advanced technology. They thought, well, I don't really know what they thought. Just that the Zulir were better. They wanted to steal the technology and make it their own. The Synnrs didn't want that. Why would we? Why start a war when technology and information were being freely given?"

"I can understand that. But racism is a hell of a drug," said Zac.

Crowze knew things weren't exactly the same as back on Zac's home world, but he'd heard enough about that place to know some kinds of hate spanned the galaxy. "That it is. After that we fought. And fought and fought and fought. Eventually the Apsyns took control of Kilrym and we got Aorsa. Every generation has a war. Some are longer, some are shorter. But we can't settle it. And I'm afraid that this won't stop until one of us gets wiped out." Crowze could remember the news reports from when he had been young. Bodies in the street, blood and fear everywhere. He didn't want that. He had joined up with the military in the hopes that he could somehow prevent it.

"Why haven't the Apsyns tried to conquer anybody else?" Zac asked. "Is it because the Synnrs are stopping them?"

"In part," said Crowze. "But they are also content to stay on their planet and revel in their superiority without needing to go any further. It costs a lot of money to conquer a planet. A lot of resources. What's the point?"

Some of the tension drained from Zac. "That's a relief at least. So it's been peaceful for the last few decades?" he asked. "How can that be if the queen was just attacked?"

"It's not just the queen," said Crowze. He had the knowledge that came from the news reports and more detailed reports that had come from the higher ups in the military. "The Apsyn prince was also attacked. But both sides claim that it was outside agitators, nothing sanctioned. It's kept the war at bay so far. It won't last."

"So you don't think any negotiation could stop this from happening?" Zac asked.

Negotiation? Crowze hadn't heard of anything like that. Could it stop things? He didn't know. He didn't want to concede anything to the Apsyns. And he knew the Apsyns didn't like the Synnrs' growing strength.

The Apsyns didn't like that Synnrs were starting to reach out to other aliens and see what it would mean to expand their presence in the galaxy. Not to conquer, but to explore. Would the Apsyns allow that? They didn't really have a choice. But a war would delay all that progress.

"You're a good storyteller," said Zac. "Somehow relaxing despite the content." Zac leaned against him with a sigh.

Crowze could kiss him. And he was pretty sure Zac would kiss him back. He had really liked doing it the first time. And he wanted to do it again.

But Crowze held back. They had time. And now Crowze was ready to do this right.

"Are you going to Solan's brother's wedding?" Crowze asked. It was supposed to be the event of the season and Crowze had not looked forward to going alone.

"I am," Zac said. "Lena invited me the other day." And then he groaned. "I don't think I have anything to wear."

"I can help you find something," Crowze offered, imagining Zac in the most stylish fashions Aorsa had to offer.

"I'd like that," Zac accepted with a small smile.

And for the first time in a while, Crowze felt hopeful. He had Zac with him. How could they get Grace?

***

"I approached you both because I want you both. Together. I was playing no games." Crowze *said it and Grace knew she had to be dreaming. She would never forget what it felt like to hear those words.*

And that time Crowze had definitely *been wearing a shirt.*

Not today. Today he wore scandalously tight pants and nothing else. He was looking at her and Zac like they were good enough to eat, the outline of his cock leaving nothing to the imagination.

There was no Simon. No queen. Just the three of them in the queen's chambers.

"We're human. Both of us." Grace had to say it, as if it was some sort of dirty secret.

"Yes, I'm very aware of that," said Crowze. If anything, his eyes got even more heated. He stalked towards her until he was too close to ignore. His hand came up to cup her face and he kissed her like there was no tomorrow.

Grace felt herself surrendering to it. And then fingers brushed her back, Zac joining in on the action. His lips ghosted over her neck and she moaned, caught between these two men and unable to get away.

Unwilling.

She didn't want it to end. Not today, not ever.

Her communicator beeped, breaking her out of the fantasy. Major Ozar. Meeting. Now. Grace wasn't sure if she should be apprehensive or not. She hadn't done anything wrong as far as she knew, but sometimes the higher-ups didn't care about that.

When Grace got there, Crowze was already sitting in one of the seats, which only confused her further. She hadn't seen Crowze since the day of the bombing. She hadn't been actively avoiding him. But it had been a relief not to see him. Not when her thoughts were still all jumbled up inside.

But she didn't let any of that show on her face. She took her seat and waited for the major to speak. "You've both been chosen for a special mission," said the major. "Highly confidential.

Highest priority. Your actions last week did you credit and you caught the eye of a certain official. Be ready."

That was... cryptic. "Do you have any more details about the mission?" Grace asked. "Even just the parameters? Infiltration? Protection?" Grace was trained in a lot of areas, but she didn't like going into missions blind. That was how people got killed.

"Protection," said the major. "Simon liked the way you both acted. You'll have more details later in the week." The major wasn't going to offer them anything else.

Grace glanced over at Crowze and saw a contemplative look on his face. He didn't ask. What was he thinking? Did he have some idea of what was going on?

"Do you have a date range, ma'am?" Crowze asked. "I'd like to be able to clear my schedule."

The major shot him a challenging look. "Your schedule is whatever I say it is." Then her face softened. "But I would suggest clearing things in about two weeks."

Two weeks to build anticipation. And hopefully two weeks to get more information.

Grace and Crowze were dismissed and they walked out of the room together.

"Any idea what that was about?" Grace asked. She hated not knowing things, which often put her at odds with her chosen career.

Crowze glanced up and down the hallway and then looked up at the security camera embedded in the ceiling. "Maybe," he said. "But we probably shouldn't talk about it here. Or at all," he added more loudly, probably trying to make sure that the security footage caught that and he was covered from being caught saying things he shouldn't be.

Grace had to hold back a smile. "Lunch?"

"I know a place," said Crowze. And she let him lead the way.

The place he knew was a little hole in the wall down the street. Grace had been there a few times and it wasn't anything special, but there was an air of privacy to the place. They took their seats and made their orders and Grace was surprised how comfortable she felt sitting across from Crowze.

He didn't say anything about the proposition he had made a few days before, but he didn't need to. The prospect of it hung heavy around them. Grace didn't bring it up. There would be plenty of time for that later.

Or not. She was still deciding.

"Are you going to the wedding?" she asked. "Solan's brother," she added after a moment. She didn't know how many weddings Crowze had invitations to. As a Synnr aristocrat he probably had plenty of functions he had to attend.

"I am," Crowze said. "I'm looking forward to it. Zac's going too," he added after a moment.

Crowze and Zac at an intimate function. Great. Because that had gone so well the last time. But things were different now. Now she knew what Crowze wanted. Now she wanted them back.

Braznon's bowels, she could just *imagine* Zac and Crowze in finely fitted clothing. Her mouth watered.

She couldn't think about that now and searched for something that would calm her raging hormones. "I was a little surprised to be invited. I didn't know Solan considered me that much of a friend."

"Of course he does," Crowze said with surprising passion. "You should have lots of friends. You're great." He smiled and it made her stomach flip. He had a decadent smile, something that promised wickedness. If she looked at it for too long she'd be burned.

Grace wasn't quite sure how to respond to that. No one had ever told her she was great before. And pretty much everyone understood why she didn't have many friends. She could be prickly, small things could set her off. She had standards, and not many people met them. But she was trying to make friends now. Trying to be better. And going to her friend's brother's wedding would maybe prove that.

And she would get to see Crowze and Zac in formal wear.

Her communicator buzzed and Grace looked at the screen, making sure that it wasn't anybody from work.

No, not work. Her breath caught and her palms started to sweat. It was a notification from the Matching Bureau. She didn't check the message. It would be rude to do that while she was out for lunch with Crowze. But her mind started spinning in circles, wondering what the message might say.

Did she have a Match?

"What is it?" Crowze asked. He glanced down at her communicator and then back up at her. "Did you just win a million credits?"

"Not sure," said Grace. She wanted to keep it a secret, and she wanted to yell from the rooftops. The two instincts warred within her. This was a message she'd been waiting *years* to get. Why did it feel weird now? Why didn't she want to share? Crowze wanted to be her friend. Her friend and more. Talking to him made sense. "It's a message from the Matching Bureau. Not sure what it says. Haven't read it yet."

Crowze's eyes widened and he sucked in a harsh breath. "You really submitted your data to them?"

"Of course," said Grace. "You haven't?" She couldn't imagine it. She had marched down to the Matching Bureau as soon as she reached adulthood and submitted to every test, subscribed to every level of Matching they provided.

She wanted a Match, and she wanted it as quickly as possible. Years later she still didn't have one. Or maybe she did. Her fingers itch to reach her communicator and read the full message. But she was going to be disciplined.

"I don't need some government database to find my Match for me," said Crowze, sounding affronted. "If I have a Match, I want to find them naturally. I want a bit of romance to it. If it's meant to happen, fate will intervene."

Of course a Synnr aristocrat would say that. "You already have your wings," she said, trying to keep her tone even, her emotions under control. "You can access your spark with the thought. You don't need a Match. Me? If I want those things, if I want to be a Synnr, I need a Match." Wasn't that obvious?

But Crowze didn't like that answer. "It is not your wings or your spark that make you a Synnr," he said. "You're just as much a Synnr as I am."

Why did people keep saying that? Were they stupid enough to believe it was true? "You have no idea what you're talking about," Grace said, anger growing within her. Of course he didn't understand. Everything in his entire life had been handed to him. Wealth, beauty, lovers, maybe even his position in the military. What he wanted he got.

And if Grace stayed here for one more second she was going to yell all that at him and ruin whatever chance they had at happiness.

The server brought their food and she asked for it to be wrapped up. "I have to go," she said. "I just remembered I have a meeting later." It was a total lie, Crowze had to know it was a total lie. But he let her escape, ego bruised and heart a little hurt.

Grace left the restaurant in a huff, feeling sick, and angry, and confused.

Why did it matter that Crowze hadn't sent his information to the Matching Bureau? Why did it matter that he wanted to find a Match organically? Plenty of people wanted to do that. Plenty of people didn't like getting technology involved. She had never begrudged them that before.

But if he wasn't in the Matching database, then whoever was listed in the communication from the Matching Bureau wouldn't be him.

Grace hadn't let herself dream of being his Match. She hadn't let herself think it was possible. But now that she knew it was impossible her heart cracked in two. Could she get into a relationship with him if she knew he wouldn't be her Match? Not all Matches were in romantic relationships. But Grace had always wanted the whole package. Wings, a spark, love. All of it.

It wouldn't be fair to start something with Crowze if it meant she was going to abandon him to some potential Match. Grace was halfway back to the training facility when she had to stop and take out her communicator. She had to know what the message said. Was she getting all worked up because they had sent a notification that had nothing to do with Matching? Had she just torpedoed her entire future?

She pulled up the information and had to read it twice to understand what it said. A potential Match had been identified, but the information was hidden. She'd never heard of that happening before.

Why would they tell her she had a Match and not give her any identifying data?

She rushed back to the training facility and found an empty room where she could call the Bureau and try and get things straightened out. She was sent through a maze of automated messages and menus and finally told that she had to fill out a series of forms and submit them to find out what was going on. They promised to get back to her in two to three *months*.

Grace almost threw her communicator against the wall, but she was trying to get more control over her emotions and merely shoved the device into her pocket.

Somehow this was even worse than having no Match at all.

Chapter Eight

What was she doing here? Grace questioned herself as she was putting on her clothes, getting into her vehicle, and driving to the beautiful facility where Ortid and Allic were having their wedding. She didn't know either man, and she was barely friends with Solan. Why was she here?

She wasn't doing herself any favors by standing off to the side and doing little more than greeting the people she recognized. It barely counted as conversation.

Why was this so hard?

Of all of the attendees, Emily had tried to coax Grace out from her hiding spot. But Grace was too much herself to let Emily get away with it. A compliment about Grace's dress had led to a sharp retort and when Emily tried to bring up their training session, tried to find some common ground between the two of them, it made Grace feel even worse.

She could still feel the sting of Emily's spark from their last training session and she didn't look forward to feeling it again.

Pretty soon she would need to start bringing a blaster or some other kind of weapon to training to even the playing field. She hadn't ever needed that against Emily and it made her feel like she was falling behind.

Of course, if she found her Match then maybe she wouldn't be falling behind for long.

The Matching Bureau still hadn't coughed up the name of her potential mate and she had filled out dozens of pages of paperwork to try and get them to reveal it. With her luck she would find out who the person was and then they wouldn't even end up being compatible.

She didn't know if that was possible. She'd never heard of a potential Match ending up false, but would people really talk about it if that happened? When people like her lived their whole lives waiting for a Match, the chance that it could go wrong would be too devastating to bear.

But Grace was just cynical enough to believe that she would be the first case of a false Match.

She had to get out of her own head.

She'd already spent a few restless nights thinking about what a potential Match could mean and she didn't need the anxiety to funnel into her days as well. But standing lonely off to the side of an event was reminding her too much of Emily and Oz's bonding ceremony. And when she saw that happy couple sneak out of the room arm in arm and head down a hallway, doubtless ready for a little private fun, she was ready to call it a night.

Until she saw Zac.

The second her eyes caught on him she found herself smiling and she didn't even realize it until her cheeks started to ache. He looked good. Damn good. He wore all black, a long jacket falling to mid thigh that came all the way up with a high collar, the edge nearly to his chin, but the shirt under the jacket opened up just enough that she got a nice glimpse of his pale skin. It was something darker than she had ever seen him wear, the contrast startling. And gorgeous. It wasn't his style, and when he tugged at the arm of the jacket and grimaced a bit, she was sure that he would be happy to be out of it.

She wanted to help him out of it. And coming up right behind him was Crowze. Oh, the things she and Crowze could do to Zac.

Seeing the two of them made her feel less alone, especially given the fact that both of them smiled the moment they saw her. They came up to her, and suddenly she wasn't standing alone in the corner. She had friends. Maybe more than friends. She had her own people.

"You look nice," said Zac. "I like the necklace."

Grace reached for the stone that hung on a long chain and gripped the cool rock. It had been a gift from her father when she graduated from the military academy. She didn't own much jewelry, but this was her favorite piece. "Thank you." Her eyes raked up and down; now that he was close she could take in the details of the embroidery. It was impossible to make out from a distance, but the jacket was stitched with even darker thread in swirls and lines and lightning. It was as if Zulir wings had come to life and hugged themselves around Zac, protecting him.

"Tell him he looks good," said Crowze, a low rumble of pleasure underscoring his words. "I don't think he believes me when I say it."

How could Zac not believe Crowze? The man was looking at him with open hunger, and if it was anyone else Grace would have been jealous. But she didn't feel jealous when Crowze looked at Zac that way, nor would she feel jealous if Zac shared that kind of look with Crowze. Especially when Crowze looked her way and nothing changed about his expression.

He wanted them both and he was no longer hiding it. Grace could get used to that.

He was addictive.

"You look very good," she told Zac. Did her voice sound different? These men did something to her and she couldn't hide her reactions.

He plucked at his sleeve again, but this time he was smiling. "I'm more of a T-shirt and jeans kind of guy," he said. "But it's nice to get dressed up for a special occasion."

"Very special," Crowze assured him.

"It's good to get dressed up," Grace agreed. "Especially when we don't need to risk being blown up." Seeing Zac in the palace, worrying for his life, had given Grace nightmares. She could handle Crowze being a warrior; that was how she'd always known him. Zac was different. He didn't belong in the heart of danger.

Zac shuddered. "If I never have to deal with that again, it'll be too soon. But this is very good. Especially now that we're all on the same page."

A shock went through Grace. She'd wondered who would be the first person to bring it up, but she wasn't surprised it was Zac. Crowze was clearly waiting for one of them to make a move. And she didn't know if she was brave enough.

"Same page, hm," Crowze mused. He looked directly at Grace and raised his eyebrows. "Are we? What does your Match have to say about that?"

So he wasn't over that. Could Grace blame him? What would she say if he had a Match? Fire roiled in her gut at the thought. Oh no, she didn't like that at all.

"I'm still working on figuring that out." Grace had to be honest. Some might have said it was wrong to be flirting with these two men when she had a potential Match out there somewhere. But she couldn't resist. Not these two.

"You have a Match?" Zac asked. He sounded... betrayed. He looked between her and Crowze and she could see a question in his eyes. But just as quickly as it appeared, it went away. Clearly Crowze was not her Match if he was asking about it.

"I have a *potential* Match," Grace felt the need to specify. She should have been jumping from the rooftops in joy. Instead, here she was with two men who weren't her Match and wishing it was one of them. Or both. "Let's not talk about this tonight," she begged. "It doesn't change anything."

"Doesn't it?" asked Crowze. He had gotten very close; she could feel the heat of his body rolling off him in waves. He should've been cool. He wore a dark blue jacket that reminded her of the sea and ice, but he was all fire. And she wanted to burn.

All three of them were huddled close together, and Grace almost missed seeing Solan and Lena sneaking down the same hallway that Emily and Oz had just left.

"The Match seems to suit them," said Zac, glancing their way for a few seconds.

"I'm not here to talk about other people," said Crowze, drawing his attention back. "The music's about to start. Will you dance with me?" He looked at both of them when he asked, and before Grace could ask him who he meant, he held out both hands.

That was how things were going to work between them. All three together. No one left out.

Things didn't get better than that.

Crowze led them out to the dance floor and the rest of the party fell away. Not literally. Plenty of people still circled around them, dancing and standing and jostling, but Grace didn't pay any attention to them.

She only had eyes for the two men dancing with her. It took them a moment to find the rhythm. But soon enough it all made sense. As long as they were all connected, all moving together, that was what they needed. At one point she ended up face-to-face with Crowze with Zac pressed flush up against her back. Oh yeah, that was good. But why did they need to be on the dance floor at all?

A nice big bed would be much more enjoyable.

One song glided into the next, and before Grace knew it they'd danced for hours. Her feet ached and she was sweating, but it was the good kind of ache, the kind that came from fun and promise.

When it was time to go she didn't want to. She wanted to take Crowze and Zac home with her and to continue the party well into the morning. But not tonight.

That didn't mean not *ever*.

She didn't kiss them. If she kissed them, there was no going home. So instead she gave them both a heated look before turning and walking away. She'd lived through battles, through training that bordered on torture. Turning away from her men was the hardest thing she'd ever had to do.

She had made it outside when footsteps pounded on the pavement and caught up with her. "Wait!" said Crowze.

Zac was right behind them.

Grace couldn't have stopped her grin if she tried. "What?"

"I almost ruined it," said Crowze, breathing a bit heavy.

"Not at all," Grace insisted. It wasn't possible. This had been one of the best nights of her life.

"Ruined it?" asked Zac. "How?"

Crowze looked between them, his spark dancing in his eyes. "I want to take the two of you out. Properly," he said. "Let me?"

Grace would let him do a lot more than that. But she liked the sound of a date. "I'd like that. I want to see where this goes."

"Yes," said Zac. "A date. Let's do it."

It couldn't happen soon enough.

***

Crowze had a car waiting for them outside of the facility. Zac wished that Grace could climb in with them and continue the night, but she lived in town while he and Crowze lived on Crowze's estate. They were going in completely different directions.

Physically, at least. Emotionally they all seemed to be headed the same way.

Crowze slid in behind him and told the driver to take off. A moment later a privacy screen slid down, separating him and Crowze from the rest of the world. It was almost startlingly intimate, and Zac found himself pressing close to Crowze, trying to feel the heat of his body and to let it seep into him.

He wanted more. He wanted it *all*. But he wanted it with both Crowze and Grace. His cock was begging him to start something with Crowze, but he knew it would be better if they waited until it was all three of them.

Why did emotions need to make things so complicated?

Crowze's presence was almost overwhelming, and when he trailed his hand down Zac's side and let it rest on his leg, Zac almost gave in. He was pretty sure Grace would understand. He had seen the way she was eyeing both of them, and he didn't think he would mind if it was just Grace and Crowze together. They were all equals in this. Whatever this was.

"We'll bring her home," Crowze said. He leaned in close and nuzzled against Zac before tearing himself away as if he was being pulled by a force that neither of them could see. Zac did his best to put a little space between them. It was harder than he expected. In more ways than one.

"Waiting makes it better, right?" he asked. "Delayed gratification?" He was reaching for anything that would convince him not to climb on

Crowze's lap and start something neither of them were quite ready to finish.

Crowze groaned, and the guttural sound made Zac's cock twitch. He let out a shuddering breath and tried to think unsexy thoughts. Long division. Alligators. Skydiving.

It wasn't working.

"Delayed gratification." Crowze tested the words, letting the syllables roll off his tongue. Zac had other uses for that man's tongue but he had to stop thinking about that. The time would come. And then the three of them would come. "We'll have our date soon enough," Crowze promised.

Thankfully the drive home was short. And a few minutes later they were dropped off in front of Crowze's mansion. The driver could've taken Zac all the way to his house, but Zac didn't mind. This way he had a few extra minutes alone with Crowze.

They walked down the path toward Human House, the air live with electricity between them. Zac wanted to reach out and hold Crowze's hand, but he didn't know if that was something the Zulir did. Would it be bad to try? He resisted the urge. Any touching was liable to lead to more touching. And kissing. And fucking. Not yet. Not now. Not until Grace was with them.

It would've been a romantic walk, if only it were dark outside. But the sun didn't set on this part of Aorsa during the summer. Zac knew he should be grateful. Come winter, it would be dark all the time. But he wanted a moonlit sky with stars sparkling above while he walked next to one of the people he was falling for.

Of course, there wouldn't be any moon lit nights on Aorsa, not even during the darkest winter. After all, Aorsa was a moon. It would be Kilrym that lit up the sky. He assumed. He wasn't an astrophysicist, and he wasn't sure how it would all work.

They made it to the front steps of Human House and both stopped. Crowze reached out and ran his fingers over Zac's cheek. Zac leaned into the touch. His whole body ached for him to get closer, for him to steal another taste of Crowze's lips to hold him over until their date.

"I should go," Zac said, but he made no move to step away.

Crowze's eyes flicked to the front door of Human House, but he didn't drop his hand. "I enjoyed tonight," he said.

"Me too." Would one kiss hurt? That was all it needed to be. A good night kiss.

No. Zac's body was strung too tight for a single good night kiss. If he got his lips on this man, he would drag him inside and have his way with him. So Zac forced himself to take a step back. "I really should go."

"Wait," said Crowze. He didn't step any closer, didn't try and hold Zac back. But Zac was frozen on the spot. "There's something I want to show you," he said.

Was that some kind of pickup line? Did Crowze want to show Zac his dick? Zac wondered if Synnr dicks looked any different than human. Maybe he could ask Emily or Lena. Or not. No, he wasn't going to do that. Was porn an option?

He had gotten so caught up in the thought that he didn't notice that Crowze took a step towards him. The alien placed an arm around Zac's shoulders and tilted his head up toward the sky. If it were dark they probably would've been looking for shooting stars or something like that. All Zac saw was blue sky. Pretty, but not quite out of the ordinary.

"What am I looking for?" Zac asked.

"Wait for it," said Crowze. His fingers squeezed Zac's shoulder and his breath brushed over Zac's ear.

And there it was. At first it just looked like a small dot, and then it came into view. A planet. It moved slowly, rising from the horizon. It wasn't Kilrym, and Zac didn't know the rest of the planets in the system to name them. But it took his breath away. More evidence that he was a long way from Earth.

Most of the time that made him feel sad. But standing in Crowze's arms, he felt hope. Things were different. There was no going home. But he had a chance to make a new life now. And he was going to grab it with both hands and hold on for dear life.

Crowze and Zac separated and shared another heated look. "Good night, Crowze," said Zac.

"Good night, Zac," said Crowze. It took another few moments for Zac to walk away, and once he was inside with the door closed behind him he let out a deep breath. He was falling for two people. And he couldn't wait to see what happened.

Chapter Nine

Synnr warriors didn't panic. Crowze kept telling himself that as he went over every single detail of the date he had planned for himself, Zac, and Grace. No panicking. He was just... confirming things. Everything needed to be perfect or his entire plan to make two humans fall in love with him was going to fail and he would be alone forever.

Not. Panicking.

It was going to go well. He didn't need to worry. After the wedding he was sure that they could make something work regardless of whether or not he could plan a perfect outing. But he did want it to be perfect.

He had applied the strategies and tactics that he'd learned in the military to plan out a campaign that was certain to hit both Zac and Grace's weaknesses. Well, maybe he shouldn't think of them as *weaknesses*. Their likes. Their desires. And if all went well he could consider it a victory.

But unlike in war, this was a victory where everyone won.

Crowze had everything set up and waiting in a nice park downtown. He could have brought Zac with him since they were coming from the same place, but they had decided to arrive separately. Crowze didn't want Grace to think that he was favoring Zac over her. It wasn't like that. He and Zac just lived near each other. And one day he hoped that Grace would join them. That he would have Zac and Grace in one big house with him. Or they could find a small one of their own. Maybe they wouldn't want to live with his entire family. He could understand that. He just wanted them with him.

Eventually. This was the first step.

Grace arrived first, but Zac was only a minute behind her. The three of them were standing on the beach near a big lake in the park and something settled within Crowze. This was right. The three of them together.

Any of that panic which he had *not* been feeling dissolved. Everything was fine. And everything was going to stay fine.

"I've lived in the city my entire life, how have I never been here before?" Grace asked, looking out at the lake. It was an oasis in the middle of the city, something not many people knew about. Crowze's father had taken him there many times when he was a child, and now he was happy to share it with Zac and Grace.

"That's a lot of water," Zac said, a little wary, a toe drawing a line in the sand.

"You afraid to get wet?" Grace teased.

Zac's pale cheeks turned a bit pink. "Everything in its time and place," he said. Whatever that was supposed to mean.

"Come on," said Crowze, ready to get started. "Let's go."

"Go where?" asked Zac. "I thought our date was happening here."

"Here-ish." Crowze nodded towards the water. "I rented a boat."

"Oh," said Zac. "A boat." He didn't sound happy about it.

Worry nipped at the edges of Crowze's consciousness. "Is that a problem?" His campaign involved a two-pronged attack. But if Zac wouldn't go on the boat, Crowze would need to figure something else out.

But Zac took a deep breath, steadying himself. "It's fine, I'll be fine."

Grace put a hand on his back to comfort him. "I'm sure we can do something else if you don't like boats."

"No," Zac shook his head, "I want to see what Crowze has planned for us."

The challenge was set. They headed towards the dock where a small boat was waiting. Crowze could've gotten something bigger, something fancier, something with servants. But he wanted the privacy of a small rowboat, something that allowed them to sit alone together and soak up the sun.

Grace took to it immediately, grabbing for the oars and rowing them out into the center of the lake in smooth strokes. It was peaceful and warm and perfect.

Except for Zac, who looked a little miserable.

Crowze was trying to think of what to do, but Grace solved the problem. She reached her hand into the water and splashed at Zac. He made an affronted noise and jumped back, almost capsizing the boat.

"What was that for?" he demanded, eyes wide.

"Have fun," she said with the air of command. "If I see you frown one more time I'm going to dunk you in the water."

"I *am* having fun," Zac insisted. He eyed the water. "But I'm a scholar. I wasn't made for sunshine and the outdoors."

Grace tipped her head back and laughed. And that's when Zac pounced, splashing her with an equally large dousing of water.

After that it was a game, waiting until someone let their guard down and attacking. By the time they had to return the boat they were all a bit drenched, but hanging onto each other and sharing smiles.

Crowze was willing to call stage one a success.

After they dropped off the boat, he retrieved a basket full of picnic foods. He held out both his arms and Zac and Grace linked up with him and let him lead them towards another part of the park, where an amphitheater was carved into the side of a hill. They took their seats as actors set up a play.

Zac snacked at first, but once the play started it held his rapt attention and Crowze wasn't sure if he remembered that he was there with Crowze and Grace.

Grace leaned close to him and laid her head on his shoulder while she ate a piece of fruit. "Thank you," she said. "This was perfect."

Crowze's heart clenched and he couldn't stop the smile that overtook his face. He leaned in and kissed her cheek. "I'm glad you could come. Both of you."

She glanced at Zac. "I think we need him. Our scholar. He balances us out. Brings us peace. He'll hold us together when we're ready to go to war."

She had a point. Crowze had never had anything lasting with a fellow warrior. He didn't know how. Sure there was sex and it was fun, but it was always competition, always battle. It couldn't last. But Zac didn't see things that way. And he made it so that Crowze and Grace didn't need to be that way either. Not when they were with him. He made it perfect.

And there was only one thing that could make this day better.

"I have dessert waiting back at my place," said Crowze once the play was over.

The heated looks that Grace and Zac gave him singed him to the core. Dessert could wait.

He wanted these humans in his bed. Now.

***

Grace's blood hummed as they pulled up to Crowze's house and he led them to a private sitting room. She'd been on his estate before several times, most recently when she was helping the humans assimilate to life on Aorsa, but this was different. She 'd never vibrated with want before while walking down a hallway.

The sitting room was nice, the walls covered in rich tapestries made of some plush material and the chairs built more for comfort than style. She appreciated that. But she did not give a *braz* about the chairs or the tapestries or any other decorations. She didn't even care about the wine and cake sitting on the little table off to the side.

She wasn't here for dessert. At least not the kind that came with food.

Zac sat down first and that's how she chose him. She was done waiting for someone to make a move. A whole day in the park was more than enough foreplay. She wanted what came next. She wanted them both.

She straddled Zac's lap and wrapped her arms around him, taking a look at him just long enough to make sure he was into this. And from the way his eyes darkened, he was. Not to mention she could feel his cock thickening between them.

She pressed her lips against his in a controlling kiss. Their tongues brushed together and her whole body lit on fire. For several seconds he let himself be kissed, but Zac was tangling with two warriors and he had plenty of dominance hidden inside of him.

His hand gripped Grace's hips and he pulled her even closer as he took control of the kiss. Grace moaned against him and let him. It was more than she had expected. Zac was their scholar. He was supposed to be the sweet one. But he was hiding wickedness inside.

She couldn't wait to see what else he had hidden.

Fingers brushed over her shoulders. Not Zac's, but Crowze's. It anchored him to them, though he didn't try and interrupt the kiss.

A minute later Grace forced herself to pull away and looked up at Crowze. His wings had flared out around him and lightning danced in his eyes. Desire. He was made of it. And he was all hers. All hers and Zac's. Just like she wanted. Crowze bent down and captured her mouth, tasting Zac on her lips. And then he eased away and leaned in to kiss Zac. Grace's core tightened as she watched them.

These two men were all hers. How had she gotten so lucky?

By the time Crowze pulled away from Zac, they were all breathing hard. The chair Grace and Zac were on was not sturdy enough for three people, and Grace was ready to get down on the floor if that's what they needed to do. But Crowze had planned the perfect date and he wasn't going to let his streak of wins end. She could see that in his eyes.

"My bed is big enough for all three of us," he said huskily, nodding towards a closed door that she hadn't noticed.

Zac twitched under her and let out a groan. "Yes," he said, the sound almost unrecognizable.

Grace stood up, but she didn't let Zac get far, pulling him up after her and wrapping her arms around him. She reached her free hand out to Crowze. "Lead the way."

Crowze did as commanded. There wasn't much interesting to his bedroom, and Grace didn't waste time looking around. All that mattered was the gigantic bed in the center. It dominated the room. It would have been obscenely large for a single person, but it was perfect for three. Lots of room for fucking, and even more for sleeping.

Not that she was thinking about sleep at the moment.

Grace stripped off her clothes in efficient movements. It was no striptease. There was no need to tease, not anymore. Not now that she had them. She wanted to be naked and under them and in between them and on top of them and everything in between. And she wanted them naked too.

"Take your clothes off," she commanded. She laid down on the middle of the bed, arms behind her head, propped up just enough to watch her men strip.

Crowze pulled his wings in and she was sad to see them go, but not sad when he stripped off his shirt and pants and revealed all of the muscled flesh she'd been dreaming about for days. Weeks.

Zac wasn't as quick to lose his clothes. He was looking between her and Crowze, cheeks pink with want and his cock tenting in his pants.

"Naked," Grace said. "Now." There was no time for blushing or shyness. Not with the three of them. "We've been dancing around each other for weeks. I want to see you."

"Of course you're demanding in bed," said Crowze. But he was smiling as he said it and he crawled onto the bed next to her, laying beside her, both of them staring at Zac. Waiting.

Crowze's hand rested on her stomach before starting to trail lower. "Do you think he needs a bit of encouragement?" he asked, the words whispered in her ear, but loud enough for Zac to hear.

Grace shivered under his touch and let her legs fall apart. "Kiss me and find out. He'll dive in when he's ready."

Maybe next time Zac would have the confidence to give them a show, but right now she would do whatever she needed to do to make sure he got naked. They all needed to be comfortable with this. She was more than comfortable, she was needy.

Crowze rolled on top of her and covered her mouth with his. She never had a chance to control the kiss, and she reveled in it. The man knew what he was doing, his mouth made for desire. She wrapped her legs around his waist and arched against him. And when she felt another set of hands touch her, she smiled.

Fingers on her ankle eased her legs from around Crowze's waist until she was laying open, and Crowze shifted to the side. It was a strange angle to kiss at, but when Zac's lips trailed up between her legs to the juncture of her thighs she knew she could get used to it. She was awash in sensation. It came just up to the edge of too much, and yet not enough. Two men worshiping her, giving her everything she had ever wanted. Everything she had never known she wanted. She would never get enough of it.

Zac might have been shy about taking his clothes off, but once his lips were on her all that shyness disappeared as his lips and tongue went to work and brought her to the edge of pleasure quicker than she thought possible. Grace writhed between them. But she still wanted more.

"You want us inside you, don't you?" Crowze asked, his lips brushing against her with every word.

Grace nodded. Her words deserted her.

Crowze seemed to like that.

"You're ours now," he said. It was a promise, but with his pleasure-drenched voice it almost sounded like a threat. "We're going to claim you. We want to keep you."

Grace moaned. From anyone but Crowze or Zac that would have made her roll out of bed right then. But she wanted to belong to them. She wanted them to belong to her. And mostly she wanted one or both of them inside her. Right fucking now.

"Zac got you ready," Crowze said, looking down at their lover as he kissed his way up her body. "He's going to take you. He's going to make you come. And then you're mine."

"Yes." Grace wanted them both. And she was done with talking.

They had to rearrange themselves, but they were so focused on pleasure that it wasn't that complicated. Zac eased himself into her while Crowze held her from behind, his lips on her neck and hands playing with her breasts. Zac captured her mouth with his own as he thrust. Her body was ready for it, almost too ready. He had brought her to the edge and back more than once and she knew it wouldn't take long for her to fall apart in his arms.

His brows were drawn together in concentration, but his eyes were dark with lust. Her scholar was determined to get this right, to solve the problem of her and make sense of it. At another time, Grace would've wondered what he saw when they were like this, but right now all she wanted to do was to feel.

And Zac and Crowze made her feel.

It didn't take him long to have her crying out, her body rippling around him as he emptied into her.

And just as Crowze promised, he took Zac's place, entering her from behind and thrusting into her with sure strokes.

His cock was different than Zac's, something Grace had known to expect. Some other day she might admire both of them, their similarities and differences, but right now she just wanted the feeling.

He started to vibrate as he got close and that was all it took for Grace to come again.

He followed quickly after her, his fangs scraping her neck, not quite enough to draw blood, but enough to remind her of the predator that lived inside of him.

He and Zac kissed over her body, and she watched, enjoying the view, before they all collapsed back down onto the bed.

She was spent, completely exhausted, and yet she wanted to do it again.

Soon. She'd had them once. And now she was determined to keep them.

Chapter Ten

Zac woke to warmth. That was his first thought. One body on either side of him, warm limbs tangled around him. Paradise. He'd slept like a baby, something that hadn't happened a lot since his abduction. But with Grace and Crowze with him he knew he was safe. Even better than that, he was content.

Grace's eyes fluttered open, but for a moment were still filled with sleep. But when she focused on him, she smiled. "Good morning," she said, her voice a bit husky.

Good? This morning was so much better than good. Zac leaned in and kissed her. It wasn't a long kiss, but it got his point across. "Did you sleep well?" he asked.

"Crowze has good taste in beds," she said with a grin.

"And bed mates," Zac teased. A look at the clock showed it was still very early, and Crowze lay beside them still sleeping. Zac would've expected their warrior to be awake at the slightest movement or sound, but apparently he trusted them to sleep beside him and felt safe enough that he didn't need to wake.

But Zac and Grace were awake. And when Grace leaned in and kissed him again he didn't hesitate to kiss her back.

Their hands roamed up and down each other, learning every inch that they could. Zac especially liked the swell of her hip and he had questions about a scar that his finger found, but they could wait. There was no need to go over a painful past at the moment.

Grace gasped as his fingers brushed against her sex, and then Zac heard a low groan from behind her.

Crowze wasn't sleeping anymore. He had cast off the blanket and his hand was slowly moving up and down his cock.

Zac would take time to appreciate the alien appendage later. The Zulir looked a lot like humans, but Crowze's cock was just different enough to be interesting.

But with Grace in his arms, Zac wasn't going to think about pleasuring Crowze. Not unless he joined the action. For now he seemed more than happy to just watch.

Grace's hand wrapped around his own cock and Zac gasped in pleasure. It didn't take long for both of them to come, and when they did they lay back panting.

Crowze was still going. And both Zac and Grace watched in rapt attention as he brought himself over with a groan.

"Now this is a way to wake up," said Grace, purring in satisfaction.

"We are at your service," said Crowze. He leaned in and gave them both a good morning kiss. But that was all it was. They needed a bit of time to recover.

"When can we do this again?" asked Zac. Now that things had begun he didn't want them to end. He might have been apprehensive about starting down this path, but after their date and their night together he knew it could work. He didn't care what the other humans thought about the relationship. As long as he was having fun with Crowze and Grace, as long as they cared about each other, what did it matter what other people thought?

But his mission for the queen loomed ahead of him. The dates weren't set, but he knew it would be happening soon. And the mission itself could take weeks. He didn't want to be separated from Crowze and Grace now that they had finally fallen in together. But he had accepted his duty.

It was one bump in the road. They would be able to move past it once they figured things out.

But Crowze and Grace were sharing a glance. Some sort of conversation was happening silently and Zac wondered if he should feel left out.

"We've been given a special assignment," said Crowze. "Not sure of when we'll be sent away or for how long. It shouldn't be too long. Not like our mission on Kilrym. But we're about to be sent into intensive training. Our time will grow limited." He didn't look happy about it.

"The queen is keeping me busy," said Zac, not sure of how much detail he was allowed to give. "Should we..." He didn't want to suggest putting things on hold now that they had just started, but what were they supposed to do? "We can just see where things go. No rush."

"The queen?" Grace asked. "What does she have you doing?" Zac probably wasn't supposed to say anything. But he hadn't been given a ton of information. He didn't think that Crowze or Grace was about to sell out Queen Serafina.

"She's made me a special advisor," he said. "I'm not exactly sure what that means. I think my job is mostly to piss off the Apsyns."

Both Crowze and Grace grinned. "Perhaps we won't be as separated as we thought," said Crowze. "And I think the three of us are determined enough to find a way to see each other."

Zac hoped so. Eventually they had to get out of bed. Crowze introduced them to his huge shower room where they indulged in more kissing and touching, and that was followed by an obscenely large breakfast.

But eventually their date had to come to an end. Crowze and Grace both had work, and Zac had studying to do. He had to learn enough Zulir etiquette so he wouldn't embarrass the queen once they finally took off.

It was going to be several days before he had a chance to see Crowze or Grace in person again. He would have to hold their night together close to his heart and keep in mind that they all wanted this just as much as he did.

By that night the doubts were creeping in. Had Zac imagined the intensity of their date? Of the passion they shared when they were together? It couldn't have been as good as he remembered. Even if only a day had gone by. And yet he was certain it was. That things between him and Crowze and Grace had been special.

Too special? Too good to be true?

Stupid anxiety. Why did it have to hit at a moment like that?

He was driving himself crazy when his communicator buzzed. He was in his room back at Human House and looking out the window towards Crowze's mansion. He wished he was there right now. He wished he was there with Crowze and Grace.

Zac answered the call. Crowze and Grace's faces appeared in two boxes on the screen. Not all of Zac's anxiety disappeared, though most of it lightened. His lovers were smiling at him and it was proof that they wanted him as much as he wanted them.

"We don't have much time," said Crowze, his face a bit miffed at the time limit." "But I wanted to say I was thinking of you both all day. And I can't wait till the next time I can get you back in my bed."

"Keep talking like that and you're going to ruin my concentration," said Grace with a heated look. It morphed into a smile. "I've got plans for the two of you."

Zac wanted to know what those plans were. There was a devious streak inside their woman and he was eager to know what she would do to them.

He settled into his bed and let the conversation wash over him. This was going to work.

They just had to find a way to be together.

***

Crowze's wings were out and ready to send his spark shooting at any assailant who would come for the queen. They had to hold the line. The door behind them was the last line of defense between the Synnr guards and Apsyns bent on destruction.

An arcing strike of an enemy's spark flashed by his head, missing him by mere inches. Crowze flinched but steeled himself. It was his job to stand between the queen and the people who would do her harm. A little spark wouldn't kill him.

But a big one could.

He shot back. It didn't connect with anyone, but it was enough to flush the enemy out of their hiding space. Another member of his team sent more spark their way.

Something bright flashed in front of Crowze, and it took a second for the pain to register. By the time he realized what happened, the simulation was dissolving around him.

Simon, the Master of the Queen's Guard, glared at him and the other members of his team. Crowze shot a glance over at Grace, who was on a different team, and she smiled back at him. They had spent every day of the last week together, but had only managed a few broken words of conversation and two comm calls sent out to Zac, who was toiling away with his own duties for the queen.

"Pathetic," Simon spat. His chest heaved and he breathed heavily, powered by the heat of his fury. "If you perform like that once we're at the summit, our queen is dead. You're supposed to be the best the Synnr military has to offer. If you're the best, we may as well surrender before any war begins."

The woman beside him flinched at Simon's vitriol, but Crowze let it wash over him. There was something riding the man, some drive that went far beyond his job. It was personal for him.

Or maybe he just took his duties very seriously. That would be required of a man in his position.

"Go take your meal," Simon commanded. "Perhaps then I'll see something worthwhile."

They scattered as they were dismissed. No one wanted to give Simon a chance to have second thoughts.

Grace caught up with him as they exited the room. She brushed against him, but they didn't kiss. They had to keep things professional during training. Crowze wanted to crowd her up against the wall and leave a mark on her, to show everyone who she belonged with.

But if his mark was there, he would want to see Zac's right beside it.

"Keep looking at me like that and we won't make it to lunch," said Grace. "And as much as I could use the break, I'm starving."

"Well we can't have that," Crowze responded.

There was a food stall just across the street from the training facility where most of the team ended up eating. Crowze and Grace found a table by themselves and sat close together.

Grace pulled out her communicator. She leaned in close to Crowze and said, "Smile," before taking a picture of the two of them. She sent it off to the message thread they had going with Zac, noting that they both missed him.

A moment later Zac sent a picture of himself with an exaggerated frown and a note that he wished he was with them.

"I didn't think it would be this hard," said Grace. She took a ravenous bite of food and chewed with gusto.

Crowze ate with a bit more refinement. Simon wasn't too hard of a taskmaster. He had allowed them meals and appropriate rest. He didn't want his team exhausted or emaciated before they ended up protecting the queen.

"We live busy lives," said Crowze. But Grace was right. Nothing had ever been more perfect than having the two of them beside him in bed. He wanted them there for good. But it was probably a little too early to make that kind of request.

There was still one worry at the back of his mind. Grace's Match. She hadn't said anything about it in several days. He didn't know if she was making an effort to find out what was going on, or she had let the matter drop.

He'd never considered himself a coward before, but in this matter he was. He didn't ask. He didn't want to know. Grace participated just as much as he did in the calls they sent to Zac. She sent just as many messages. She seemed to miss him just as much as he did.

And she had kissed him with breathless passion the few moments they'd managed to sneak alone. They hadn't done more than kiss. Not with Zac gone. Perhaps one day things would work in any variation of their group. But not until things were more settled between them all.

"Do you think we can sneak away before the mission?" Grace asked. "Just for one night. One more night with the two of you before…" She didn't say if she was worried about things going wrong. Things could go wrong on any mission. But Simon's training tactics were a bit more brutal than most, and both Crowze and Grace had died in several of the scenarios he had put forward. It was a stark reminder of what could happen in their line of work.

Crowze wasn't afraid of death. Not most of the time. He couldn't do his duty if he was. But he didn't want to lose Grace to the fire of an Apsyn spark. He didn't want Zac to be blown up because security had failed.

"I'll take any time with you that you can give me," said Crowze. He reached out and squeezed Grace's hand. He would've kissed her if the other people weren't around. The relationship wasn't exactly a secret, but if he kissed her right now he didn't think he would stop.

Grace picked up her communicator and sent a message to Zac. It only took a few seconds for him to respond.

Grace grinned. "It looks like we're on."

Crowze leaned in and gave Grace a quick kiss. "It can't come soon enough."

Chapter Eleven

The building didn't look like much of a hotel, but Zac wasn't sure what he expected. He was living on an alien moon after all. He headed straight for the room, the number having been sent to his communicator.

Grace and Crowze were supposed to be waiting for him, and anticipation thrummed in him. He'd spent the last week learning as much

Zulir decorum as a person could possibly learn and etiquette was bleeding out of his ears.

He'd had enough of that. He didn't think he would embarrass the queen; at least he hoped he wouldn't. But maybe she wouldn't be too upset if he did. After all, he was there to make the Apsyns uncomfortable.

He put those thoughts out of his mind. The summit would happen soon and there was nothing he could do to stop it or speed it up. He didn't need to worry tonight. Tonight he just got to spend time with Grace and Crowze, one last date before they all had to focus on saving the world.

He was comforted to know that Grace and Crowze were part of the team that would be guarding the queen and him. He trusted them with his life.

And his heart. Maybe it was too soon to be thinking in the long term, but Zac was all in. Had been since before their first date. So much of his new life didn't make sense. But him, Grace, and Crowze did in a way he'd never thought possible. He was going to do whatever it took to keep them.

Zac knocked on the door when he got there. For a moment, he didn't hear anything, but then the lock started to turn and the door was opened by Crowze.

The warrior smiled when he saw Zac and Zac leaned in to kiss him. He hadn't even thought of it, it felt so natural. And when they separated, Crowze was grinning.

"It's good to see you in person," said Crowze, closing the door behind Zac and leading him into a small hotel room.

It was strangely familiar. A large bed, a small sitting area, a window that looked out over the city. How could he be so many light-years away from Earth and yet sitting in spaces equivalent of a Holiday Inn?

It was things like that that gave Zac pause sometimes. Those little reminders of home. Of Earth. It made him wonder if he wasn't actually in space, but in some coma or something back in South Bend. He didn't think he was in a coma. Then again, he couldn't prove otherwise.

It was something he didn't let himself worry too much about. If this wasn't real it was still real enough. And he didn't know if he could've dreamed up Crowze and Grace.

"What's that look?" asked Crowze. He took Zac's overnight bag and set it beside his own.

"Just wondering how all of this is real," said Zac. He might have tried to hide his flights of fancy from someone else, but not from Crowze, not from Grace. He trusted them.

"I assure you, it is," said Crowze. He gestured to a small table that was covered with snacks and beverages. "If you're hungry."

Zac was hungry all right, but not for food. "Where's Grace?" he asked. This night together had been her idea. He wasn't disappointed to have a few minutes alone with Crowze, but he was here to spend time with both of them. At first they had planned on some kind of outing, but it quickly became apparent that they just wanted to spend time together. This hotel room, this oasis in the city, was exactly what they needed.

A strange look passed over Crowze's face, one Zac couldn't quite interpret. "She had an errand to run," said Crowze. "She promised she'll be back soon."

"Did you come here straight from training?" Zac asked. From the messages and calls they'd exchanged, it was clear that training was its own kind of torture, and Grace and Crowze ended most days exhausted.

"We did. Grace left only a few moments before you arrived."

"Did you have any fun without me?" Zac asked with a smile. The sheets didn't look rumpled, but there were plenty of other places they could've gotten up to mischief.

And there was that strange look on Crowze's face again. "No." He paused, approaching the table and grabbing a small bottle filled with clear liquid. Probably water. He took a sip. "We discussed it. Not today, a few days ago. But as we haven't established what is acceptable to you, we didn't do more than a little kissing."

Zac's heart swelled. He would be lying if he said that he hadn't felt alone over the past week, separated from Crowze and Grace by his duty. Knowing that they thought of him, that they had considered his feelings, was a strong reminder of how they were in this thing together. "You and Grace, you and me, me and Grace, as long as it's the three of us there I'm good," said Zac. "I'm sure we'll figure this out."

Crowze took a seat in the small sitting area and Zac grabbed a bottle of water and joined him. Something was bothering Crowze and before Zac could ask, he spoke.

"Grace hasn't said anything about her potential Match. I haven't asked. I don't know how." His vulnerability was staggering. Zac could see his fear and doubt on his face, his emotions completely naked.

The fact that Grace had a Match out there somewhere concerned Zac, too. Would she be stolen away from them by this mysterious person? Or could she somehow manage their relationship and a Match? "Ignoring it won't make it go away," Zac had to point out. It never worked.

"What about you?" Crowze asked, piercing him with the question.

"What about me?" Zac didn't follow.

"Are you interested in getting tested for Match compatibility? Do you want to know if you have a Match out there somewhere?" The words were sharp, but not quite stinging. This was something that must have been bothering Crowze for some time.

Zac shuddered at the thought of more tests. "Between what they did to me on Kilrym and the tests the queen told me I had to take before the summit, I would be happy to never be tested again in this lifetime. Apparently I'm healthy, that's all that matters." When he and his fellow humans had arrived on Aorsa, they had almost been forced into tests for Match compatibility. As far as Zac knew the test wasn't particularly invasive, but he didn't like the idea of his information just sitting in a database somewhere. "At least the queen promised confidentiality. I don't want to be anyone's lab rat."

"What tests?" Crowze asked. "I didn't realize that was part of your mission."

Zac shrugged. "There was a stack of paperwork about a foot high that I had to sign," he said. "But after a while I stopped reading. I know it's bad. But what was I going to do? Say no to the queen? Yeah, that doesn't seem like a good idea. I mean, she's very nice to me. But she's the queen. So I just signed everything and let them do what they wanted. They told me how I could access my results, but by that point I wasn't paying any attention." He figured if he had some sort of weird space disease they would tell him; he was too overwhelmed to deal with anything else.

Crowze stared at him for a long moment. Zac felt like he was under a microscope again. What was Crowze thinking? Before Zac could ask, the door opened and Grace came in.

All three of them together. Finally. Just as it was supposed to be.

***

Grace dumped her bag of clothes beside the two bags already on the floor. She was supposed to take them to work with her, but a slight mishap in the morning left her without an overnight bag. She had rushed home as quickly as possible and was only delayed by her mother, who wanted to talk. She knew all about Zac and Crowze.

Grace hadn't been able to keep quiet about it. She was happy. She didn't quite know what to do about that, but for the moment she was going along with it. She deserved a bit of happiness.

Of course, her mom didn't know about Grace's potential Match. Other than Zac and Crowze and the Matching Bureau, Grace hadn't mentioned it to anyone. It seemed useless to talk about something before she knew if it was even real. Or if she really wanted it.

And if she talked about it, someone might want her to make a decision. Might want her to leave Zac and Crowze, or to turn away from a potential Match. She wasn't leaving Zac and Crowze. But she couldn't quite give up the dream of her wings. Not when she'd wanted them her entire life.

But she wasn't going to think about that now. Not when Zac and Crowze were looking at her with alarming levels of intensity. She had barely put down her bag when her men got up from their chairs and stalked across the room towards her.

She hadn't suggested a night together just for sex. Their day boating and going to the play had been one of the best days of her life, and that still would've been true if she hadn't spent the night in Crowze's bed. But all three of them were about to embark on a dangerous mission and they needed this affirmation that they were in this together.

Crowze kissed her first, his arms coming around her and pulling her flush up against his body. It went on just long enough for her to become breathless before he pulled back and guided her towards Zac.

Zac's kiss was sweeter, not tentative, but gentle. She could get lost with both of them. She wanted to.

Fingers teased the bottom of her shirt and started to guide it up, exposing her stomach to the warm air of the room. From the angle of the hand, it had to be Crowze who had managed to work his way behind her. He eased the shirt up and over, breaking her kiss with Zac, before throwing her shirt away. It landed somewhere. She didn't care where. Once she was naked, none of them were putting on clothes until morning. Zac and Crowze shared a kiss over her shoulder, both of them pressed tight against her. Both cocks hard.

Grace could get used to the feel of being between both of them. She wanted to.

It became a blur of kissing and touching, of sensation and pleasure and every promise that this relationship could bring. They tore at each other's clothes, removing them with a desperate haste that spoke to the week they had been apart.

Things between them all were still too new for the separation. And when this mission was over, Grace wanted to find a way to hide out for weeks on end with no one but her two men beside her. Did it sound like an impossible dream? Yes, but anything felt possible with Crowze and Zac.

The pleasure of their lips and hands was almost too much to bear. And by the time Grace was lying down on the bed, her heart was beating wildly, legs splayed, and full form on display for her men.

It was different than last time. More sure. More intense. It almost felt like Zac and Crowze had something to prove. Like they wanted her to know that she belonged to them.

She did.

Crowze crawled between her legs and laid his lips on her. Grace arched up into him and stared at his dark hair as he feasted on her. Zac moved behind him and she was confused for a moment as he bent down, but when Crowze gasped against her she realized what was going on. Crowze wasn't the only person feasting on another. And he was bringing Crowze a different kind of pleasure.

It went on and on, her fingers tangled in the sheets under her, and the anticipation was so much that it was almost painful. How did people survived this much pleasure? She didn't know, but she still wanted more.

Crowze stiffened under her and pulled away from both her and Zac. "I don't want to come yet," he said. His fingers gripped the base of his cock, which was already twitching in pleasure. It wouldn't take much before it started to vibrate, and once that started it was all over. There was no stopping the orgasm once a Zulir cock was ready.

Zac's lips were red and his eyes a bit dazed. "We have plenty of time for act two," he said. His voice was lower than she had ever heard it, drenched in pleasure and promise. Had she ever thought Zac would be shy in bed?

She couldn't have been more wrong. Perhaps the first time together he had a bit of an issue getting naked, but that time was long gone.

"Inside her," Crowze ground out. "Together."

At first Grace didn't realize what he was talking about. But when she did she couldn't hide the moan that escaped. "Yes," she said. "Yes. Together. Now." She'd never done it before. Hadn't really thought much about it. But now that Crowze suggested it, it was exactly what she needed.

Zac's nostrils flared. If he had been Zulir, lightning would've been dancing in his eyes. But today Grace didn't see that as a deficiency. He was human. Beautifully human. And all hers. Hers and Crowze's.

But just because she wanted it didn't mean she was ready yet. Her body was strung tight, on the edge of orgasm, and when Crowze's fingers found her folds it didn't take much to bring her over. But that was only the beginning. He let her catch her breath for a moment before stretching her out even further.

"There's lube on the table," Crowze told Zac. "Get her ready."

Zac took the instruction well and a moment later, Grace felt fingers against her ass. It was strange at first, and she was already so full. What would it feel like when both of them were within her? She wanted to know. She wanted it now.

"I'm ready," she insisted. "I want you inside me. Both of you."

"Are you sure?" Crowze asked. He was the one who'd suggested it, but now he seemed ready to take a step back. "We don't have to do this tonight. There will be other times."

She was done wasting time, done doubting. "I want you both. Now." Did she have to write it on a banner?

No. Now they were ready.

They got into position, Crowze in front of her, Zac taking her from behind. And though her body wanted hard and fast, Crowze took it slow. Easing himself all the way inside her until they were fitted together. Then he looked at Zac. "Your turn. Go slow."

The head of Zac's cock brushed against her ass, and as he pushed inside slowly Grace started to wonder if this was the best idea. She felt a burn and a stretch, and it was almost too much. But she was a Synnr warrior, she could take a little pain. Especially when she knew it was going to pay off.

And after a moment her body surrendered to the stretch. And then Zac was pushing beside her. Once she was accustomed to him, Crowze took his turn, easing himself inside her, filling her to the brim. Making her whole. Crowze kissed her. Then Zac. And then Zac kissed him. And then they were all moving together. Joined as three people in one body.

They treated her with care. Almost too much care. But this was the first time, and Grace could appreciate it. Her body would be sore in the morning. Probably more sore than she'd ever been. And she longed for it. She longed for the memory of the two of them imprinted on her long after they had to separate.

Already primed with pleasure, it didn't take long for her to shudder around them, coming again. And soon after that, the heat of her body and the tightness that came from two cocks inside her was enough to have Crowze and Zac emptying themselves within her.

They rested after that. And cleaned. And the lovemaking the rest of the night was gentler. An affirmation of their connection.

As Grace went to sleep, she was more confident, more sure that these were the two men for her. No matter what else happened. No matter what the results of any Match compatibility test said. She belonged with Crowze and Zac. And that wasn't going to change.

She was ready to sleep the night away beside them both. But the world had other plans. Sometime in the very early hours, her communicator started going off madly. And then so did Crowze's. And then shortly after that, Zac's.

It was time to report for duty. The summit was on.

Chapter Twelve

Crowze and Grace had to find Zac on the space station where the summit was being held. He had flown up with all of the diplomats while they were stuck with the guards. The flight had taken only a few hours, but Crowze missed Zac all the same. Everyone had a little bit of time to settle in before they had to get to work, and Crowze intended to steal a few moments with his partners.

He didn't know how long they would be stuck on the station, didn't know how long it would be before he could have them in his bed again. And though his body was sated from the night of lovemaking, he wished he could have them again right now.

But there was work to do.

Still, he couldn't be begrudged a few minutes.

"Two humans? Save some for the rest of us," said one of his fellow guards.

Crowze gave the man a playful shove and didn't otherwise respond. He knew a few of his fellow soldiers didn't understand his fascination with humans. Crowze wouldn't call it a fascination, though, he just didn't see the difference between human and Zulir. He happened to want two humans. It didn't matter that they didn't have wings. That they didn't have access to their spark. That wasn't what he was attracted to.

Those soldiers didn't appreciate the sharp bite of Grace's wit or the beauty of Zac's smile. They didn't know what it felt like to lay between the two of them and know true contentment.

When Crowze started down this romantic path, he hadn't realized that this relationship was something he would want for the long-term. But now that he had both Grace and Zac, he wasn't going to let them go.

He only hoped Grace's mysterious Match didn't screw everything up.

He put that out of his mind. He wasn't going to waste these minutes he had with Zac and Grace on sour thoughts.

Zac was looking around their wing of the space station, eyes wide and mouth open in fascination. He had never been on a space station before. Crowze hadn't realized it until just this moment, but that was the only thing that explained it. Sometimes he forgot that Zac had a completely different upbringing, that Earth was nothing like Aorsa. And then there were these moments where Zac was fondling one of the walls, his finger tracing over a seam in the metal so gently, like he was afraid that it would crack in two if he touched it too hard.

"You like seeing him like this," Grace observed, coming to stand next to him.

Crowze dropped his hand and let it brush against Grace's arm. They weren't keeping their relationship a secret, but he doubted she would appreciate if he started clinging to her in the middle of an assignment. "Can you say any differently?" he asked.

"He makes me think of this world differently," she said. "He sees things that I stopped looking for a long time ago."

That was one way to put it. Crowze took his life, his world for granted. Even standing on the edge of war. But it was all new to Zac.

"What kind of metal is this?" Zac asked, now touching it with a bit more vigor. "Shouldn't it be cold?"

Crowze had no idea what he was talking about. He placed his own palm against the wall and was surprised to find it neither warm nor cold. "I don't know, do you?" he asked Grace.

"I'm a soldier, not a scientist. Or a construction worker. How would I know?" Grace smiled as she said it.

Zac had a thoughtful look on his face and Crowze was sure he was making a mental note to do more research about the space station. "What about gravity?" Zac asked. "How does that work up here."

"There's a gravity drive," Grace explained drolly.

"What does that even mean?" Zac pressed.

Neither Crowze nor Grace could explain it. It was just something they were used to having.

"Captain Kirk would know," Zac muttered.

Crowze and Grace shared a look. Captain Kirk? The only captain with them right now was Simon.

"Is that one of the guards?" Grace asked, looking back to where a group of them were still clustered further down the hall. "I don't remember meeting someone named Kirk. But I could have forgotten."

Zac burst out laughing. "No, I'm sorry. Captain Kirk is a character from a television show. Star Trek. He's not real."

Crowze wanted to ask more about this Star Trek, but Grace beat him to it, a smile of recognition blooming on her face. "I know about that," she said. "I think my mom mentioned it. She used to watch it when she was a kid."

Crowze couldn't remember hearing Grace speak fondly of anything from Earth, of anything human. He was happy to see her bonding with Zac over this small thing. He wanted her to be proud of who she was, of where her ancestors were from. He didn't know how to talk about it with her. He didn't know if he should. She was as much of a Synnr as he was, but she was still human. She always would be. And he wanted her to accept herself.

But time was running short. Crowze and Grace had to go get ready to speak with Simon, and Zac would have his own duties. Crowze and Grace both took turns kissing Zac before he had to go.

They both knew it could be the last kiss for a while. They would have to be on good behavior now that the Apsyns would be around.

Crowze watched him go, but he wanted to call him back. Wanted to kiss him again. Wanted to take both him and Grace and find an isolated corner somewhere where they could spend the next hour ignoring their duties.

But they couldn't. They were all too responsible for that.

This mission couldn't be over soon enough.

***

Grace knew that nothing exciting would happen before tomorrow. Today they were getting accustomed to the space station and setting out guard routines. Tomorrow would be the first official diplomatic meeting where the queen and the Apsyn prince would begin testing each other for weaknesses. This meeting was meant to stop a war, but it had an equal chance of starting it.

Grace was just ready for *something* to happen. Synnrs and Apsyns had been dancing around one another for months. Years, really. The holding pattern had everyone anxious. Peace or war, they needed it now.

Grace and Crowze were at a planning meeting with the rest of the team. Simon stood in front of everyone and was going over the layout of the space station, and the roster of both the Synnr and Apsyn delegations. The space station had multiple wings and the Synnrs had control of one while the Apsyns were taking another. Neither of them would be manning the control room. However, both delegations would have guards standing there. Just to stop any funny business.

It all seemed simple enough. Unless this was one giant ambush, Grace expected things to go smoothly. But a not-so-small part of her expected an ambush. How could she assume anything else? Apsyns were assholes. And if they could strike at the queen, could take her out, it would be a huge victory. It would be a declaration of war.

She hoped that wasn't the plan.

After giving them a holographic tour of the space station, Simon switched the holo display to show the members of the delegation from Kilrym. For a moment, Grace was confused.

Were they looking at the diplomats or the guards?

"I realize they all look like bruisers," said Simon, nodding towards the images. "I've had extensive research done on every document given to us from the Apsyns. Every single ID matches up. As far as we can tell these are legitimate diplomats."

Grace peered at the display. What kind of diplomat was as big as a warrior? She could understand one or two, but all of them? That seemed a little strange. She didn't like it.

She glanced over at Crowze and he caught her gaze. He raised his eyebrows, silently communicating that he was just as doubtful as she was.

She trusted Simon. And Simon doubtless had plenty of spies down on Kilrym who could find the information that they needed. But the Apsyns had spies of their own and were equally capable of creating false identities for a handful of soldiers posing as diplomats.

It was too late to do anything about it now. Every single Synnr guard chosen for the mission would be on alert. They had backup stationed on a ship not very far from the station. If they needed help, help could come.

But she didn't like the feeling that they were walking into a trap.

Simon continued the meeting, going over information about every Apsyn and Synnr on the station. That included every guard in the room.

She committed every face to memory. If someone tried to lie about who they were, she wasn't going to let that happen.

She didn't have wings, but she wasn't going to let that stop her from doing her job.

The meeting took a little bit more than an hour, and at the end of it assignments were handed out and they were all dismissed. Grace was happy to see that she and Crowze would be sharing quarters.

Crowze and Grace headed towards their room. "What do you think about those diplomats?" she asked.

She and Crowze were far enough down the hall that none of the other guards could hear them. Not that it was a big deal. So what if they were overheard? They were all on the same side. And the Synnr guards needed to be on alert.

"They could be legit," Crowze said, but he didn't sound too sure. "I suppose if they are retired military or something like that. But I can't say that I have ever particularly trusted the Apsyns."

There was no such thing as a trustworthy Apsyn. "Simon chose us to keep the queen safe. Let's do our job."

Chapter Thirteen

It felt like the night before a big test. One he hadn't studied for. Something with a lot of math. Zac was an English major. He didn't do math. And that continued on into grad school. English literature. Not algebra. And yet he knew that tomorrow he would be dealing with some insane sort of calculus that he had never seen before.

His stomach was in knots, and even though he was in the communal cafeteria he wasn't sure he could force any food down. And cafeteria wasn't exactly the right word—no Queen would eat in the cafeteria. There were a lot of tables set out at intervals and food set up in plain sight of everyone. But servants brought it to them. And guards from both the Apsyn contingent and the Synnr contingent flanked the table to ensure that no one tampered with the meal.

At first Zac thought that all of the Apsyns in the room were from the guard contingent. They were all over six feet tall and their muscles had muscles. They were like the gym guys Zac had seen lifting weights whenever he managed to hop on a treadmill. Big and intimidating and full of testosterone.

He supposed someone could say the same about Crowze, but Zac wasn't intimidated by him.

He didn't see anything alluring in these Apsyns. Not when he had seen the darker side of what their society had offer.

But could these muscular guys really be the diplomats? There were a few women around too, just as muscular as the men.

It felt wrong.

Fishy.

He was sitting at a table with the queen and Simon, but was far enough away that he couldn't say anything without being heard by half a dozen other people. He didn't want to raise his concerns to the entire room. And he definitely didn't want to be overheard by the Apsyns.

Zac just kept observing.

He noticed the way two of the Apsyns who were sitting at their own table surveyed the room. If someone walked in, their eyes found that person immediately and tracked them as they made their way to a table. If there was a loud noise, one of them looked towards it while the other kept his eyes on the other half of the room, as if looking for some kind of threat.

Diplomats were attentive, but not like that. Those men were soldiers.

They had to be.

And where was the prince?

The Apsyns were supposed to be sending a prince to negotiate with the queen. It was possible he was tucked away in his own quarters right now. He might've had someone bring him a meal.

The queen had opted to eat in public as a sign of strength. As a sign that she was not afraid of the Apsyns, and as a sign of goodwill. She wanted her people mingling. Wanted them to prove that they could really move forward with their diplomatic aims.

If the prince wasn't here he did not think the same.

Was he here?

Simon would know. But Simon was sitting beside the queen and Zac didn't think he had the right to ask.

The Master of her Guard looked confident. Then again, the man always looked confident. He wouldn't let anything show if he thought that something would go wrong.

Zac looked around, hoping for a familiar face. Other than the queen, he didn't have any friends among the Synnr diplomats, and he didn't know who he could bring his thoughts to.

Maybe he would have to tell Simon if he could get the man alone for a minute.

He wished that Crowze and Grace were with him. Those were two people he would tell without hesitation.

He didn't know if he was right. He hoped he was wrong. But Grace and Crowze would listen to him. They would take him seriously. And if his fears were founded, they would be in a place where they could do something about it.

But they weren't here. A few of the Synnrs were on guard duty, but clearly Crowze and Grace were not at the moment. He didn't know if they were guarding somewhere else, or if they were preparing for tomorrow. He wished he could send them a message on his communicator, but he'd had to surrender that when they got to the space station.

He needed to talk to them. Needed to figure out if things were really as bad as he feared. Or maybe this was just anxiety from his first diplomatic mission.

Hopefully his only diplomatic mission. He didn't want to fail, but he didn't think that this was his true calling. He just needed to get through the next few days without massively screwing anything up.

But he had a feeling that everything was about to go horribly wrong.

***

The quarters that Crowze and Grace had been assigned had plenty of room. The space station was quite large. Though it was costly to get materials into space, once they were up there, the station wasn't confined by any of the building constrictions that could hamper construction on Aorsa or Kilrym. It meant that he and Grace were not shoved into a tiny closet and forced to sleep in bunk beds.

The furniture could be arranged in several different configurations, and Crowze eyed the beds, pretty sure that they could be pushed together to make room for both him and Grace together.

And Zac. But Zac would have quarters of his own. So close to them and yet separated by metal and space.

Their things had been delivered directly to the room and they both had clothes in the drawers and the small closet.

Crowze began changing out of his outfit almost as soon as the door closed behind him. He and Grace weren't on duty for several more hours, and while they couldn't completely relax, they could be a little less formal behind closed doors.

Grace apparently had the same thought. She unbuttoned her jacket and put it to the side before reaching for the hem of her shirt and pulling it over her head. Crowze forgot what he was doing. He watched as the dark material disappeared to reveal the pale skin of her stomach, her breasts still covered by a utilitarian bra.

It shouldn't have been sexy. He had seen plenty of his fellow soldiers dressed in exactly the same clothes before. He had seen *Grace* like this many times before they were more than just coworkers.

But now they were more. And now it meant more. And now his cock wanted in on the action.

He reached down and readjusted himself before things got uncomfortable and then leaned back to watch as she got undressed the rest of the way.

It took Grace a moment to realize he was watching her, and when she did she paused and looked over at him. "Enjoying the show?" she asked with a grin.

Crowze flicked open the button to his pants and let his hand dip inside, teasing over his cock. "You know I am," he said.

Grace made a show of it, wiggling her hips as she took off her pants and taking her time to strip out of her bra. Crowze wanted her to stay like that the rest of the night, but he knew she wouldn't. There was still a small chance they would be called back to duty, and she wouldn't want to be caught with her pants down and shirt off. He couldn't blame her. But he could enjoy it while it lasted.

He pushed off the wall and stalked towards her, crowding in close and backing her up and halfway into the closet.

His hands landed on her hips and held her close, reveling in the feel of her warm skin under his fingers. "That's better," he said. "Like this."

Grace leaned in close to him and nuzzled against his neck, pressing her body against his. "I don't know if we're supposed to do this." She let her lips brush against his neck before pulling back a little. Not out of his embrace, but enough to put a hand's width of space between them.

"Are you worried Simon will call?" Crowze asked. He didn't want to have to rush anywhere with a throbbing cock. And if the teasing was bad now, he could only imagine how much worse it could get. He could take it. It was worth it. But he didn't need all those levels of frustration.

But that wasn't what Grace was worried about. "I know we talked about it a little, but Zac's not here."

No, he wasn't. And Crowze could feel his absence just as much as Grace did. He reveled in this time alone with her. He wanted to kiss her now and to take her to bed. He wanted to lose himself inside of her. But without Zac there, a piece of them was missing. It would be good. But not whole.

"We don't have to do anything without him," Crowze said, even if his cock did *not* agree to stopping things. "But you know I wouldn't be jealous if it were just the two of you. Though I would appreciate pictures."

Grace was grinning even if she shook her head. "It's one thing to say that when we're separated by a city, but Zac is just down the hallway somewhere. I would invite him here, but we took away all the communicators." She reached behind herself blindly and grabbed for a shirt. Crowze was disappointed to see her put it on, but she had a point. Zac should be there with them.

But that didn't mean they couldn't kiss. Once the shirt was over her head he leaned in and captured her lips. He kept it chaste. Or as chaste as it could be when it was the two of them. He had her back completely up against the closet, his hips pressed against hers, when someone knocked at the door.

Crowze pulled back with a curse. They were supposed to be alone. They were supposed to have some privacy.

They weren't supposed to be on duty until tomorrow.

The person knocked again.

"You better answer that," said Grace.

She pushed him towards the door and went in search of pants.

Crowze had to take a deep breath to calm down. But he supposed it was for the best. If he and Grace got much further, it would be a frustrating night for both of them.

***

Crowze's hair looked like fingers had been running through it and Grace's shirt sat strangely, as if she had hastily pulled on. They'd been making out. Zac was sure of it. Satisfaction pooled deep within him at the thought. His only regret was that he hadn't been there to see it.

But all three of them couldn't be together all the time. He knew imagining them would be enough to light a fire in his dreams for weeks to come.

But Zac wasn't there for sex. No, he needed advice, needed to talk to the two people he trusted most in the world. In all of the worlds. The galaxy. It was strange to consider how fast both Crowze and Grace had taken up that position for him. But they had. And he was a lucky man that he could turn to these two people.

He stepped into the room and closed the door behind him. It was bigger than he expected. He had known that the space station would not resemble the space stations from Earth. The Zulir were much more technologically advanced than humans. At least when it came to space travel. The structure really was like something out of Star Trek: huge, a bit industrial, and fit for a crew of hundreds, if not thousands of people. He was just glad he wasn't wearing a red shirt.

His own quarters were big as well, but meant only for one person. The bed that Crowze and Grace had laid out was easily big enough for three.

Zac thought in that number now. Three. Either a bed could fit all of them or it wasn't good enough.

He had to focus. He was here to talk about the job. Not wonder if they could manage to snuggle together.

"It's good to see you," said Grace. She had managed to straighten out her shirt and was leaning back against the wall. Arms crossed. "But shouldn't you be in a meeting or something? Lots of important things to discuss."

Zac rolled his eyes. "I'm pretty sure that I am purely decorative. And there are no meetings right now. The important stuff is supposed to start tomorrow." Zac started pacing and discovered the limitations of the room. He only got four steps in each direction before he had to turn around. And on his second pass, Crowze got in his way and placed both hands on his arms to stop them.

"What's going on?" he asked.

Zac leaned into Crowze for a moment, sharing in his strength before he pulled away. He had to be strong enough to talk on his own. If he couldn't talk to Crowze and Grace, he couldn't talk to anyone.

"Something feels *wrong* about this whole thing," said Zac, finally letting himself feel all of his worries. "I know I don't have a lot of experience, any experience, with this sort of thing, but it feels... like a trap." He hadn't let himself think that word. He hadn't wanted to consider it. But that was what this was. "The prince was not at dinner tonight," he continued. "The queen showed up. Our diplomats showed up. But if the people the Apsyns claim are diplomats actually are, I'll eat my hat."

"What hat? And why would you eat it?" Grace asked, face scrunched up in confusion.

"Do you even have a hat?" Crowze asked.

Zac let out a sound of frustration. "It's an Earth saying. It means that I'm sure I'm not wrong." Zac flopped down on the bed and bounced a little as the mattress sprang back. "The alleged diplomats all look like bodybuilders or soldiers. Not just *look* like them. I saw the way they were looking at the room. Scanning for threats. They were like the freaking Terminator."

"Terminator?" asked Crowze.

"I know that one!" said Grace with a smile. "It's an evil robot."

"Cybernetic organism, technically," Zac corrected out of habit. And he wasn't going to go into the entire Terminator mythos right now. They had more important things to discuss. "I'm not saying that they're cyborgs, but they're dangerous."

"I had the same thought," Grace agreed. "About the danger, I didn't consider that they could be cyborgs."

"Do cyborgs exist?" Zac asked. He knew it wasn't the time, but he kept learning so much about his new life, and he couldn't help but be curious.

"Not among the Zulir," said Crowze. "But I'm sure there are cyborgs somewhere out in the universe."

"Don't need to be cyborgs when you have magic powers," Grace said with a hint of wistful sadness.

Zac and Crowze shared a look, but they didn't say anything. They would have to talk to Grace about her attitude toward Synnrs and their spark eventually. But not today.

"Did you tell Simon about this?" Grace asked. She pushed off the wall across the room to take a seat in one of the chairs. "He's the one who'll want to know if anything is wrong."

Zac grimaced. "No, I haven't. I wasn't sure. I don't want to bother him with a false alarm." Now was not the time for his anxiety to flare up, but Zac couldn't help it. He was still the new guy in town and he still felt out of place.

But neither of his partners held it against him. Crowze just nodded as if he had expected that response. "We will keep our eyes open," he promised. "If the Apsyns are up to something we'll see it. And we will report anything suspicious to Simon. You don't have to worry about that."

"I'm not worried about it," Zac said. It was true. "Not when I know you two are here." If he had the choice of an entire army or just Crowze and Grace, he would probably still choose Crowze and Grace. Maybe it wasn't the wisest choice. Maybe he shouldn't let his heart and his cock make those decisions, but he had. And he wasn't going to regret it.

"We will protect the queen," Grace promised, face solemn and eyes serious.

That had only been a small part of why Zac had come to the two of them. Sure he wanted the queen protected. Sure that was Crowze and Grace's job. But there was more to it than that. "I'm worried about the two of you. I love you." He hadn't quite been looking at either of them as he said it. So Zac turned to Grace and met her eyes. "I love you," he said to her. And then he turned to Crowze. "I love you."

They were both frozen in place and Zac wondered if he had overstepped. Everything had happened so fast between the three of them, and yet it felt as natural as anything in his life ever had. Maybe they weren't there yet. Maybe they didn't feel the same. Maybe he had overestimated what this relationship meant to the two of them.

The doubts tried to assail him, but Zac pushed them away. He knew that Crowze and Grace were dedicated to him. He knew that they wanted him.

If they didn't have the words, they would find them.

Eventually. He hoped.

But he didn't know if he could stick around for much longer if they just stayed quiet like that.

Zac pushed himself up from the bed. "I should probably go."

Crowze was closest to them. He took a step towards him and placed a hand on his arm. "Stay. There's room enough for all of us."

It wasn't a declaration of love. But it was enough.

Zac stayed.

Chapter Fourteen

Crowze couldn't tear his eyes away from Zac. He had never had anyone tell him that they loved him before. He'd had plenty of lovers. But nothing like this. Part of him was at a loss. What was he supposed to do? He would give Zac his very soul if the man would take it. Well, half of it. The other half belonged to Grace. But the words got caught in his throat. They didn't feel like enough. But if Crowze couldn't tell Zac, he would show him.

He only hoped that Grace felt the same way.

If she didn't, she would. He was certain of that. She was already falling for them. She already felt something. But he wanted his humans to feel everything.

Crowze might've been lost for words, but Grace wasn't. She sat forward in her seat, and the movement caught both his and Zac's attention. "I want to watch you," she said. "I want to see what you could do to each other."

Crowze's cock stiffened and he glanced sideways at Zac, whose pale cheeks had grown pink at the thought. Yes, Crowze liked the thought of that. Putting on a show for their woman. Getting to feel Zac beneath him. They might be sitting in a space station on the verge of having a trap sprung up, but tonight could still be perfect.

Zac stepped towards Crowze. After he made his declaration, he had seemed ready to bolt, but now his confidence had come back. He shot a cocky grin at Grace. "Any special requests?" he asked as he came up behind Crowze and laid his lips on his neck.

Crowze leaned back into him, enjoying the feel. He was a sensual man, one who enjoyed being touched, and touching. And he wanted to revel in the feel of Zac against him.

They were both watching Grace and her smile grew wicked. "Make a game of it," she said. The queen might've been staying down the hall, but Grace looked resplendent, as if she were sitting on a throne of her own. "Whoever lasts longer gets me."

Had Crowze been hard before? That made him even harder. "So you're a prize to be won?" he asked. He'd take her over all the riches in the world.

"You know I am," she said. Then she nodded towards the bed. "Get to it."

Crowze's concentration was split in three ways, and somehow that seemed to heighten the whole experience. He wanted to bring Zac as much pleasure as possible, wanted him writhing beneath him and delirious with desire. And he wanted Grace begging for it by the time he was done. But he also had to keep an iron grip on his control. He didn't want to lose. Not just because he wanted to lose himself inside Grace, but because he wanted to bring Zac to the heights of pleasure as well.

And he was competitive. It came with being a soldier. This was better than any war he could fight.

Crowze backed up into Zac before turning around and pushing him towards the bed. Zac stepped back without any resistance, but when Crowze pushed him, Zac grabbed on tight and pulled Crowze down with him.

They landed together in a pile of limbs and Zac kissed him like there was no tomorrow. Their tongues clashed and danced together. It was on the edge of violent. But the kind of violent that came in bed. No weapons needed here. Nothing but lips and teeth and skin and cock. Zac's hand quested between them and dug into Crowze's pants, circling around his hardened length and making him moan.

Crowze was supposed to have more control than that. And a quick fumble on top of the bed would be no show for Grace.

Crowze tore himself away, regret laced in every inch he put between them. Zac's eyes followed him as he slid back till he found the catch of Zac's pants and undid it, pushing them down to reveal his hard human cock. He looked different than Crowze, human instead of Zulir. But Crowze liked the variety. And he liked any part attached to Zac or Grace. Crowze got his lips around Zac and used his tongue to torture him, swirling around the head and licking his length in bold strokes.

Zac thrust against him, the sounds he made primal. He wouldn't last long. Crowze was sure of that. He was going to win.

But thoughts of any sort of competition, of any sort of prize, fell away as he brought Zac pleasure. He wanted to give his man this. Wanted to give all of himself. It wasn't about control or a prize or anything but Zac.

And though Crowze forgot the reason they were there, Zac didn't. He pulled away, fingers circling the base of his dick. Face full of frustrated regret. "Not so fast," Zac gasped, cheeks flushed. "I'm not going to make it that easy."

He pulled Crowze up and they kissed again. Zac had to taste himself on Crowze's lips, but he didn't seem to mind. And after a few moments, Crowze found himself on his back and now it was Zac's turn to kneel before Crowze and take him in his mouth.

It was unstudied at first. Clearly Zac had never licked a Zulir cock before, but what he lacked in experience he made up for in enthusiasm. And it wasn't long before Crowze was thrusting into his mouth, lost to the pleasure that Zac was giving him.

He heard Grace moan and opened his eyes to look at her. She had her shirt off and pants unbuckled, one hand disappeared into the dark fabric. She was enjoying what she was watching just as much as he enjoyed feeling it.

And Crowze remembered the goal. He needed to make Zac come. He wanted to bring both of his partners to pleasure. It was his purpose in life.

He tore himself away. It wouldn't take much to bring him over. But if he was that close, then

Zac had to be in the same spot. All he had to do was get his lips back around Zac's cock and it would be over.

Zac's lips were swollen and his eyes dark and heavily lidded. He looked utterly debauched, absolutely delicious. It was almost enough to send Crowze tumbling over, but he bit the inside of his cheek, that little bit of pain giving him enough control.

But Zac played dirty. It was a filthy game.

He came up behind Crowze, kneeling behind him on the bed, his cock teasing Crowze's ass as his fingers wrapped around Crowze's penis. "Do you see her there," Zac whispered in his ear, his voice raspy and full of desire. "Those fingers of hers playing with her cunt. Imagine us inside her. Remember the heat of her wrapped around us at the same time. The way she gripped us as she came." Zac squeezed as he stroked and it was enough; Crowze couldn't help it as pleasure exploded through him and he erupted in Zac's hand.

Zac kissed him roughly and laid him down on the bed. Crowze watched, still drunk on pleasure as Zac turned toward Grace and stalked over to her. "You're mine," he said. If Crowze had any stamina left in him that would've been enough to set him off again.

***

If Zac looked back at Crowze he was going to come. He was balanced on the edge of orgasm and would tip over with the slightest hint of sensation on his cock. Even looking at Grace, cheeks flushed, chest heaving, was almost too much. Part of him was shocked his words had worked. He had never been one for dirty talk before, but Crowze brought it out of him. And his memories of both of them buried deep inside their woman.

He bit his tongue to distract himself. He hadn't come this far only to disappoint Grace. Crowze was panting on the bed. Zac wanted to leave Grace in a similar state.

He needed to buy time. Time to get himself under control. He had never before wished he was wearing a cock ring, but now he saw the appeal. Maybe some other day. But not right now. Nothing short of an enemy attack could pull him out of this room.

And even then it would need to be a pretty serious attack.

With the confidence born from bringing Crowze off, Zac decided to try out his new talent on Grace. He got up close, but kept just enough space between them to leave her aching to close the distance. "Did you like that?" he asked, lips brushing over her ear. "Liked seeing my hand around his cock, liked the way he surrendered to it. Do you want to taste?" Zac had managed to wipe most of Crowze's come off of his hand, but there were still a few drops. He put his fingers in front of Grace's mouth and she sucked hungrily.

Zac groaned. If he was trying to get his cock under control that was a terrible idea. And yet he didn't pull away. Not until his fingers were clean and Grace was moaning for more. He pulled his fingers out of her mouth and cupped her chin, closing their mouths together in a searing kiss. There was something more primal with Grace and Crowze. Something darker, harder than Zac ever had before. He felt like he was unleashing some sort of beast that lived deep inside him, something he hadn't even realized he'd been keeping caged for all these years.

He loved it. He loved them.

He kissed his way down her neck and took a moment to pay attention to her breasts, twirling his tongue around her nipples and teasing them with his teeth. Not enough to hurt, just enough to remind her of where she was, of who she was with. And then he was kneeling between her legs, working her pants down and all the way off before kissing his way back up and seating his mouth at the heat of her sex.

Grace moaned and arched, pressing harder against his mouth. He feasted. His tongue delved deep into her folds, reveling in her taste.

Her fingers fisted in his hair, keeping him in place, exerting control over him. He didn't know if she realized what she was doing, what it felt like, but he didn't care. As long as it was her he loved it. He would happily take her commands as long as she was willing to give them.

And the rest of his body loved it too. His cock hadn't flagged at all since he'd approached her, but he was pretty sure he was no longer seconds from detonating.

Zac replaced his lips with his fingers, teasing her and preparing her. "Are you imagining what it looked like when I was laying there with Crowze?" he asked. "Are you imagining his taste? You haven't had your lips around his cock yet. Only tasted his come."

She moaned, and a masculine moan came from behind them. Crowze had recovered enough to watch them, and his hand was gently playing with his cock, not quite bringing it to full hardness, but not leaving it to suffer. His wings were out, glowing bright in the dim room and reminding both Zac and Grace that he was not human. They were beautiful. He was beautiful. Zac wanted to go over there and feel those wings, to revel in their electric touch. But he didn't know if he would be burned.

He turned back to Grace. "Look at him," he commanded, his fingers delving inside of her, stretching her. She moaned again but looked over at Crowze. "He's on display for us," said Zac. "He wants us to know that he's with us even when he doesn't touch us. Our beautiful Synnr warrior." Grace gasped. She was close. Almost as close as Zac. He needed to be in her. Now. There was another chair not far behind him and he pulled back, taking Grace with him. With her on his lap, it didn't take much to get his cock to tease her entrance. And now that she was on top of him, she was in control. Just like they all liked it. She eased down, filling herself up until they were joined completely together.

They looked over at Crowze and watched as lightning danced in his eyes.

Zac's question about his spark was answered when Crowze sent out a gentle lick of electricity towards them. It tickled Zack's skin and made goosebumps rise on his flesh.

It made Grace move even faster, bouncing up and down on him as the spark mixed with both of them. Zac moved in motion with her kissing and touching, sparing glances for Crowze. All of his senses engaged. Grace danced above him, her body rippling around him, and that was all he could take. With a groan he emptied himself inside of her.

They stumbled over the bed a few minutes later and all ended up in a pile together, sharing gentle and not so gentle kisses. It wasn't going to go anywhere else. They were all spent from a late night the night before and an early morning, and from the certainty of the terrors to come.

"We will keep you safe," Grace promised as she drifted off to sleep.

Crowze kissed him before succumbing himself.

Zac hoped it wasn't necessary. But he had a feeling that everything was about to go to hell.

Chapter Fifteen

The Synnrs and Apsyns were congregating in a large room set up for diplomatic talks. Their guards had been commanded to stay outside of the room. It was meant to promote a sense of trust among all the diplomats. Instead Zac just felt more wary. He wished Grace or Crowze were in here with them. Simon would be useful too.

Really, any of the guards. He still couldn't help but notice just how big all of the Apsyn diplomats were, and still the prince was nowhere to be found.

Something was wrong.

Zac still hadn't told the queen or Simon anything. Was it really his place? Now Grace and Crowze knew. And if they were in here with him he knew they'd be seeing the same thing he was. But they were stuck outside. Somewhere.

An Apsyn who was slightly less muscular than the rest of them entered the room. Zac could have believed that this guy was a diplomat, but he didn't trust the rest of the Apsyns as far as he could throw them.

The Apsyn came up to the queen and gave a slight bow. "Your Majesty, my deepest apologies. My name is Ren. I have been assigned to speak on the prince's behalf."

The queen's expression didn't change, but Zac could already hear whispers starting among the rest of the delegation. "Where is the prince?" she asked, her voice dangerously neutral.

Ren bowed again. "He was unavoidably detained. He begs your pardon. And he promises that I speak with his complete authority."

"His complete authority?" Queen Serafina challenged. "So if these talks were to end with a marriage between my heir and his, you have full authority to consent to the match?" The queen seemed taller, less frail. Zac didn't know what they'd done to her to make her seem so healthy. She was recovering from her wounds, but today she looked stronger than he had ever seen her. It was almost unbelievable.

Ren stuttered and could not agree to what the queen said.

"As I thought," she said, stabbing him with each word. "If your prince cannot bother to show up to prevent a war, why should I talk to you? Get your prince. He has until tomorrow to appear. If not, we will be leaving." The queen did not turn and walk away. She refused to cede any ground. After all, Ren had approached her.

And he backed away with as much haste as a man could.

Zac had to reveal his suspicions now. With the prince definitely gone, nothing good could come of this situation.

None of the other Synnrs seemed willing to get close to the queen at the moment. Did they fear her wrath? He hadn't known her to be an angry woman, though he couldn't say that he knew her very well. But given that the room was still half full of Apsyns, Zac did not expect her to make a scene.

"Your Majesty," he said.

Queen Serafina made a sound of frustration. "This is low even for them," she said. "I expected them to make impossible demands. Not to pull a stunt like this."

"Are Apsyn diplomats usually so large?" he asked. He couldn't be the only one who'd noticed it. Grace had. "I'm not saying that muscular people can't be smart or diplomatic, but I'm fairly certain that most of them cannot bench press a car."

That startled half a laugh out of the queen, and she had to snap her mouth shut to keep from making more undignified sounds. "You might have a point. If my diplomats looked like the Apsyns, I think I would be accused of starting a harem."

"That's not my worry," Zac said. Though for a moment he had an image of one of the Apsyn diplomats feeding grapes to the queen as she lay on a particularly plush couch with the other ones massaging her feet and fanning her with giant leaves.

"You think they're planning something?" she asked, though it was more statement than question.

"Don't you?" Zac shot back.

The queen considered it. "Perhaps. But this is bold even for the Apsyns. I need to speak to Simon. Go get him."

"I can do that." Zac wasn't much of a negotiator, but he was more than capable of running errands.

As he turned to walk away, the queen summoned another one of her diplomats over and designated her to act as the queen's voice until the prince arrived. The queen couldn't talk to any of the lower ranking diplomats in her official capacity. She was too important.

Zac wanted to ask her if it was really safe for her and her people to wait in the same room with the Apsyns, but he didn't turn around. She was a smart woman who thought tactically. If she wanted to stay in this room, there was a reason for it. And she and more than half of her retinue were Zulir. Even without weapons they weren't completely helpless.

But Zac walked quickly. He wanted Simon with her as fast as possible.

The halls were empty and ominous. Zac could feel the weight of the place, though that might've just been the artificial gravity. But anticipation hung in the air. Something was about to happen. Maybe it already was. Did the Apsyns have space ships lined up around the station, ready to shoot, to take out the queen before she could escape? He didn't doubt it. But he knew that Simon was in communication with their backup. If Apsyns were making moves around the station, Simon would know about it.

Zac sped up, breaking into a run. It would probably look suspicious if anyone caught him, but Zac didn't care. Not right now.

He burst into the small office that Simon was using as headquarters and Simon spun around, his face filled with worry. His eyes roamed up and down, checking Zac over for any wounds. And as soon as he was certain that Zac was fine, a mask of professionalism came down over Simon's face.

"What is it? What are you doing here?" Simon demanded in staccato syllables.

Zac relayed his suspicions to Simon as quickly as possible. Telling him the prince had not shown up, talking about the size of the guards, and saying that the queen had sent him.

Simon considered all of Zac's words, but he didn't look nearly as worried as Zac was. "I've confirmed the identities of every single diplomat on the station. Both Synnr and Apsyn. I know how to do my job."

Zac was sure of that. And he didn't want to challenge the man, but Simon had clearly missed something. "Can't identities be faked?" After all, the Synnr military had managed to get Grace to infiltrate an Apsyn research center with a fake identity. Why couldn't the Apsyn diplomats do the same?

"Yes," Simon conceded with a grimace. "Of course that's possible. But my sources are very good."

Zac doubted they were good enough. He didn't say that part. But it must've shown on his face.

"You don't understand how things work here," Simon told him, clearly reading Zac's look. "I will lay down my life and more to keep Queen Serafina safe."

Zac didn't doubt that. And they did not have time to fight. He backed off as much as he could. "The queen needs you," he said. Simon straightened, something Zac hadn't realized was even possible given how straight his posture already was.

"No guards are allowed in the diplomatic room," Simon said. "Breaching that agreement could have dire consequences."

The prince hadn't shown up, the consequences were already dire. But Zac didn't say that part. He glanced around, looking for some idea. His eyes snagged on the ID badge hanging from his shirt. Zac grasped it, tugging it off and handing it over to Simon. "Take this. Say you're me."

Simon took the card gingerly, but he wasn't convinced. "We look nothing alike."

That was true. But Zac could recall how the Apsyns had treated him and his fellow humans when he'd been held captive. They had barely been able to tell the men and women apart. Sure, Simon was a bit taller than him and much more muscular, but they were both human. "Humans are below their notice," Zac said. "They don't think we're people. I don't think they can tell us apart."

"If they catch on, it will have repercussions," said Simon.

"This thing has already gone lopsided. And if the Apsyns attack, you need to be with the queen." Zac was doing everything but shoving Simon out the door. He wasn't a warrior, he couldn't protect anyone. How did Simon not see it?

Apparently he did. He took Zac's badge and took off.

Zac was left alone in the office. And he realized he now had no ID badge. Maybe he should have asked for Simon's in exchange. He didn't know what the consequences would be if someone found him without a badge of his own, and he was not eager to find out. He also couldn't go back to the diplomatic room if Simon was going to show up and say he was Zac.

The best thing to do right now was head back to his quarters and wait things out. Hopefully things wouldn't go all to hell while Zac waited.

He took a turn towards the Synnr quarters, but before he could make it even a few steps two Apsyns blocked his path, each of them looking incredibly sinister.

They didn't give him a chance to talk or fight. Zac saw a flash of white and then everything went black.

Chapter Sixteen

Crowze and Grace were patrolling the halls for trouble. So far they had found none. Nothing. The halls were strangely deserted. Though there was probably no reason for the diplomats to be out in the halls when they were supposed to be negotiating.

Crowze still expected to see some people. They should have crossed paths with other Synnrs and perhaps with a few of the Apsyns.

There were just as many guards as there were diplomats, and the space should have felt crowded rather than deserted.

Instead it was like he and Grace were the only two people on the space station.

He couldn't help but think of Zac's suspicions. Was something wrong? Was Zac right about this being an Apsyn trap?

He could've been. Dread pooled in Crowze's stomach at the thought. He was torn in two directions, wanting to protect Zac and knowing it was his duty to protect the queen. Luckily the two of them were supposed to be in the same place right now. Protecting one would protect the other.

He wanted to say something to Grace, but they both needed to be watchful. This was no time for conversation.

Footsteps pounded towards them and Simon came rushing around the corner. He paused for just a moment. "Keep on alert. I'm going to see the queen."

He didn't let them ask questions, didn't pause long enough for that. Grace and Crowze watched as he continued down the hall and then they shared a look.

"Should we follow him?" Grace asked. Her body was turned in that direction and it would only take a word from Crowze to have them rushing after Simon.

What had Simon heard that had him going that way?

"Not quite yet," Crowze said. If something had tipped Simon off, he and Grace could be back up. They didn't need all of their forces huddled together, easy pickings for Apsyn troublemakers.

They kept moving on their guard rotation. The hair at the back of Crowze's neck prickled and he let his wings flare out one moment before something crashed down on his shoulder. It would've been worse if his wings weren't out. And still it hurt.

He whipped around, sending his spark flying towards the enemy.

Two Apsyns stood behind them, both with their wings out and wicked looking batons in their hands.

Grace already had a blaster out and was firing towards them, but the Apsyns were skilled warriors and were able to use their wings to deflect the blows.

They kept shooting off their spark when they could and Crowze heard Grace gasp out in pain and tumble over. As she crashed to the ground he wanted to cover her, to make sure she was okay. But she would not be okay if he didn't get rid of the threat.

He lashed back out with his spark, but it wasn't enough to fend off two Apsyns. They stopped shooting their sparks at him once he ended up on the ground as well. They closed in, evil looks on their faces, each gripping a baton and eager to hit.

The first blow hurt. The second was worse. After that they all kind of blended into one another.

Was this the end? Was his life really going to be ended by two Apsyn brutes on a space station far from home?

It wasn't supposed to go this way. He had only just found Zac and Grace. He wasn't ready for it to end.

One of the Apsyns grunted and stumbled back. Crowze heard flesh pound against flesh and then the telltale crack of a blaster. The second Apsyn was distracted and Crowze summoned his spark, blasting him at close range and sending him sprawling.

Grace stood behind him, chest heaving, a blaster in her bloodied hand. He pushed himself to his feet before she could offer him a hand up.

"I think that answers whether or not something's wrong," Grace said, the words coming out a little winded. Half her face was swollen and her lip was split.

"We have to warn everybody," said Crowze. They had to go back to where all the diplomats were. They had to follow Simon and find the queen.

But Grace was shaking her head. "Med kit first. You're bleeding. So am I. We'll be of no use to them if we faint from blood loss. I think there's one just down the hall."

Crowze wanted to argue. But Grace had a point. Whatever the Apsyns were planning, it was already underway. And they would be useless if they walked into a fight already half-defeated. At the very least they could slap on some healing gel and take a couple pain suppressors. Then they would be ready to fight.

They rushed down the hall. There was a sign on a closet door that indicated it had supplies and a med kit inside. Grace tested the handle and cursed when she found it closed.

"There's got to be another one," said Crowze. If they didn't find it quickly they would have to head back without tending their wounds. They couldn't waste too much time.

Grace looked down and froze. Then she crouched and Crowze followed her gaze. There was a streak of blood on the ground and it cut off right at the door.

"Someone was dragged inside there," she said, mouth set in a thin line and eyes grim.

They couldn't force the door open by pulling on it, but Crowze had learned how to pop an electric lock with his spark at a young age. It was a trick plenty of Synnrs loved to pull. And as soon as the lock disengaged, the door swung open and revealed Zac slumped over against the wall, an ominous pool of blood next to him.

Grace gasped and then made a sound like she was choking on a cry. But she recovered her emotions quickly.

"Come on, help me. We have to get him out of here." Zac's clothes were all torn and bloodied and there wasn't a bit of him that didn't look bruised. He was in bad shape. He needed a doctor or a med bot. Or a miracle from the med kit.

Grace took one of Zac's arms and Crowze took the other. They pulled him out and laid him down in the hall. Then Grace reached over and grabbed Crowze's hand, as if she needed the emotional reassurance that they were all together.

But the second her bloodied hand touched his own, their blood mingling, a shock of recognition tore through him.

A Match.

***

White flashed behind Grace's eyes, and for a moment she thought she was dead. She wasn't sure what would meet her in the afterlife, and

213

when her brain had a second to catch up to what she was feeling, she realized she still didn't know. She wasn't dead.

She had a Match.

Two Matches.

But Zac was still bleeding and moaning in pain, and she had to ignore the life-changing implications of what she'd just found out for the moment. She left him lying there next to Crowze for a moment and rushed back to the closet to find the med kit. Zac was a mess, but with some healing cream, a pain suppressor, and the stimulant, he should be on the way to mending. Or at least as mended as he could be before they got him to a doctor.

He needed to be okay. And it had nothing to do with the fact that he was her Match. How was that possible? Shouldn't she have known?

She had spent her whole life hoping for a Match and now it looked like the two men she was in… involved with might just belong to her in that most visceral way.

It was too good to be true. She couldn't believe it. She couldn't even think about it without her hands shaking.

Crowze was strangely silent. Not that he was the most talkative man at the best of times, but this silence was strained. He kept glancing at her and then back down to Zac, wiping away at his bloodstained skin with a bit of damp gauze and not daring to say anything.

Why wasn't he saying anything?

Did he not want this? Was he in shock? Or was he just concerned for Zack's well-being?

That's were Grace's thoughts should've been, not scattered all around the place and wondering what was going on.

Zac groaned again, louder this time. He was coming back to consciousness, the stimulant doing its job. And Grace felt bad for him when the groan of awareness turned to a groan of pain.

With Crowze's help, Zac was sitting up. He put a hand to his head and breathed deep for several moments before he spoke. "What happened? What's going on?"

Everything was going on. Grace couldn't sum it up quickly. She needed a day or a week or a month to get it all sorted out in her own mind.

But Apsyns were causing trouble and they did not have time for her to be conflicted.

"It looks like you were attacked," said Crowze. "So were we. Apsyns." He paused, and for a moment Grace thought he wasn't going to say anything else. But then he glanced over at her and then back at Zac. "And when Grace and I pulled you out of the closet, all of our blood touched. We're a Match."

Zac blinked several times, as if he was trying to process all of that. Then he started to nod his head slowly and looked over at Grace with a big smile. "It looks like you get your wings," he said.

Grace's heart cracked. This was supposed to be everything she ever wanted. Everything she ever wanted wrapped up with the two guys she wanted. Her wings, her loves, a whole life laid out together in front of them. She didn't have to worry about some random stranger being a partial Match for her. It should have been perfect.

But it felt all wrong. She felt like she was standing on the edge of the biggest decision she would ever have to make. She didn't want to force Zac or Crowze to bond with her. She didn't want them to have to make this decision right now. So why did it feel like they were barreling towards it?

"We need to think about this," she said. She crossed her arms and half turned away. If she could've run, she might have. She didn't run from battle, but this was a war she didn't know how to fight. Who was she even fighting?

Crowze stood up and got close, but he didn't quite touch her. Did he think she would run? He wasn't far off. But the warmth of his body steadied her and she leaned in against him. She didn't want to run from these two. But did she really deserve them?

"We don't need time," said Crowze. "I know what I want. I've wanted it for a while now. And the fact that you're both my Matches is just further proof that we all belong together. I would never force you into anything. Neither of you. And you know that. But—" he slammed his mouth shut and shook his head, not continuing the thought.

She knew what he didn't say. They were heading into battle against a bunch of Apsyns who were ready to fight. And it was possible that most of the Synnr guards had already been incapacitated. A Matched unit was more powerful than any single Zulir. If she and Zac had wings and access to their sparks it might just turn the tide.

She wanted wings so desperately she could practically feel them against her back. But was that why she was leaning towards agreeing? Was that fair?

"What about that potential Match?" she asked. They didn't have time for this. She knew that, but it had to be said.

"Were you tested for Match compatibility before coming up here?" Crowze asked Zac. He put his arm around Grace's shoulders, giving her the comfort she craved.

Zac was still reeling from the assault and it took him a minute to think. He shrugged. "I don't know. I suppose it's possible."

"If Zac was tested at some sort of royal facility, maybe there was more privacy than usual for his test results," Crowze guessed, but it left Grace feeling even more confused. "Maybe both of you were in the system as a partial Match, but because you're both human, or because it's all three of us together, it didn't show as a complete Match. We can find out later. Does it really matter?"

It really didn't. Maybe the Matching bureau had been wrong. Maybe some clerical error somewhere had cast confusion over them. They had the proof in their blood right now, far more convincing than any digital message could ever be. Grace knew they were hers. All she had to do was agree.

"I don't want to force Zac into anything," she said, finding her last excuse. He had only been on Aorsa for a few months. She couldn't take these decisions away from him.

"I told you about how I felt last night," said Zac. "My feelings haven't changed. I want to be with both of you. All the way. Whatever that means."

"If you don't understand—"

Zac cut her off. "I've been here long enough to understand what this means. I have friends who have been Matched. And I am old enough to make decisions for myself." He looked over at Crowze.

"Matching gives you a power boost, doesn't it?" he asked.

Crowze nodded. Zac struggled to his feet, and both Crowze and Grace helped him up the rest of the way.

"If the Apsyns are causing trouble, we need all the help we can get. That's not why I'm saying yes to this," he was sure to point out. "But it's why I'm saying we shouldn't talk about it anymore. I'm in. Are you?" He met Grace's eyes as he said it.

Something settled within Grace. Zac's confidence, his certainty. The strong feel of Crowze beside her. This was how it was supposed to be. The three of them together. All the way. She wasn't sure why she was rejecting it. She was scared to get everything she had ever wanted, perhaps. But she couldn't let that fear rule her. Especially not now when they were sitting on danger's edge.

"Let's do it."

Zac grinned. Then the grin slid off his face. "How?"

This Grace knew very well. She had spent half her life studying what it meant to have a Match and how it was done. The knowledge might've been theoretical, but it was simple enough. "We each have to pull power from one another," she said. "I reach deep into the both of you and summon your spark to use as my own. You both do the same. Once we've all done it, the bond is sealed. And there's no breaking it after that."

"Good." Zac leaned in and kissed them both quickly. Grace caught the disturbing taste of his blood, but he seemed to be recovering more and more by the second. Zac didn't give them a chance to back out. He closed his eyes and took a deep breath. And then Grace felt something yank from deep within her. She gasped as Zac reached for her spark and pulled it towards himself until lightning danced between his fingers.

"Whoa there," Grace warned. "A little warning next time. And maybe a bit gentler."

"That's not what you said last night." He was brimming with excitement and electricity and it was infectious.

Crowze was more gentle. She felt the brush of his spark against hers as he summoned her power and Zac let out a little gasp, feeling the same. Sparks flew out of Crowze's fingers.

It was Grace's turn. Once she was done there was no turning back.

It was easier than she expected. She summoned her concentration and reached for both of her men, finding the power and grabbing a handful of it from each of them. Her spark lit up deep within her, igniting for the first time in all of her life and making her blood fizz.

She sent out a crack of power and the bond was sealed. She looked over and saw bright blue and orange wings erupt from Zac's back and her breath caught. She could feel the ghost of the weight of her own wings. Nothing physical, but real all the same. Crowze leaned in and kissed her. "Stunning," he said when he pulled back. "I always knew you would look good with wings."

Grace couldn't stop the smile that blossomed on her face. Wings. She finally had her wings. "Let's go kick some Apsyn ass."

Chapter Seventeen

Crowze could feel his bond to Grace and Zac deep within his blood. He wanted to roll around in it. Feel their sparks against his skin and bones. But there was no time for that. The Apsyns were up to something, and the queen needed them.

They took off running towards where the diplomats were supposed to be gathering. Given that they had all already suffered Apsyn attack, they knew they needed to get the queen off the space station and back to the safety of Aorsa.

Crowze only hoped that the Apsyns didn't have the station surrounded. Getting off the station could be just as dangerous as staying on if that was the case. They had to want to capture her. Holding her hostage would be much smarter than killing her out right. If she was alive she was a bargaining chip; if she died it was an act of war.

The other diplomats wouldn't be so lucky. They had some level of importance, but probably not enough to keep the Apsyns from killing them.

Clearly Zac and Grace felt the same urgency. They were outright sprinting through the halls, and it must've been luck that prevented them from running into other Apsyns. Or the Apsyns were busy causing trouble somewhere else. Crowze wasn't sure which he wanted to be true.

They made it to the room and Crowze was sure they were too late.

"My God," said Zac as he looked over the chaos. Two Apsyns were slumped in a corner, either unconscious or dead. A Synnr was on the other side of the room, also unconscious, but Crowze could see the subtle rise and fall of her chest. She was alive. Good.

"No queen," said Grace. They looked around quickly, just in case something was obscuring the queen from their view, but that didn't appear to be the case.

"Do you think Simon got to her in time?" Zac asked, full of fragile optimism. He looked at Crowze and Grace hopefully.

"No way to know," said Crowze. He didn't want to quash Zac's hope, but he wouldn't lie to the man. "Given that there was a fight, it suggests we weren't completely helpless." And Simon wasn't lying dead—of course, Crowze didn't say that part out loud, but they all knew the Master of the Guard would've laid down his life before he let the Apsyns take the queen hostage. Since he wasn't here it was likely they hadn't grabbed her yet.

Crowze hoped that was true.

"We have to keep looking," said Grace. Both Crowze and Zac agreed. But once they were back in the hallways they moved more cautiously. They followed a trail of blood and destruction, passing by an Apsyn body and an ominous pool of blood. This was all evidence of battle.

So where was everybody?

An Apsyn almost got the drop on them, coming out of nowhere and shooting bright arcs of his spark their way. Without pausing to think about it, Grace summoned her wings and sent her own spark sizzling back at him. The Apsyn dropped to the ground in defeat.

Grace let out a whoop of excitement and grabbed onto Zac's hand. He was closest. But she only took the second to celebrate the use of their new powers.

"We have to keep going," she said, but Crowze could still hear the strain of excitement in her voice.

They came around the next corner and there was Simon, standing proud, blaster pointed and ready to reap destruction on whoever came his way. His eyebrow was busted open and blood trailed down the side of his face. He looked like he'd been beat up, but he was alive and standing.

"Friends, Your Majesty," he called out. And a moment later, the queen stood up from behind a pile of haphazardly stacked crates.

"Good." She made no comment about her undignified hiding place. And no one else said a thing. "We need a report," she said.

"We found the meeting room in shambles," said Crowze. He didn't make excuses or try to say that the queen and Simon had to know more than he did. All information needed to be gathered at this moment. "Apsyns appear to be roaming the halls. This place isn't safe."

"Yes," Simon agreed. "We need to get the queen to safety. There is a small cruiser in one of the hangars. It's more secure than the escape pods. It comes equipped with a defense shield. Get us to the hangar."

That snapped the three of them into action.

They weren't far, but it soon became clear why Simon wanted the extra cover to get to the hangar. The queen was limping badly, and after only a few dozen feet Simon had to pick her up and carry her the rest of the way. He couldn't defend her and carry her.

Luckily, none of the Apsyns found them. They took enough time to confirm that the small cruiser hadn't been tampered with before getting the queen and Simon inside. Crowze, Grace, and Zac might have joined them; unfortunately the vehicle only sat two.

"If there was any other way, I wouldn't leave," said the queen. It was a nice thought, but she had to get out of there. She was too valuable to remain. If the Apsyns captured her, they'd win the war before it started. "We will send for reinforcements the moment we are able. Stay strong."

"The escape pods will probably be safe enough," Simon told them. "There are many of them all over the station. We're close enough to Aorsa that you should be able to pilot one home. If not, you can send out a distress signal. But the Apsyns will be listening for those as well. Be careful."

He sealed the hatch of the cruiser and Zac, Crowze, and Grace retreated out of the hangar so that the bay doors could be opened.

"Sounds like it's time to get out of here," said Zac.

Crowze wasn't sure it was the best idea, but there were no good ideas right now. And he didn't want to be stuck on the station with a bunch of violent Apsyns.

They turned back the way they came on the assumption that there would be fewer Apsyns that way. A shadow fell across their path and Crowze was ready to lash out, but a Synnr came around the corner, one of the diplomats. "Apsyns are attacking," he panted. "They want the queen."

"She's safe," Grace promised. "Get to an escape pod. Get out of here. There's no use trying to hold the station."

The Synnr didn't try and stay with them. He took off and Crowze and his companions soon followed.

Another Apsyn crossed the path and Grace tried to use her spark, but this time she couldn't access it. It took practice to figure out how these things worked, and Crowze was ready to step in, but this time Zac was able to summon his wings and send a blast of power at the Apsyns. It was enough to push him back, but Crowze used his own spark to finish the man off. It was more power than he'd ever summoned, and he didn't even break a sweat. He could get used to this whole bonding thing.

They passed an empty escape pod, but something had been done with it to prevent it from launching.

The next option had already been launched.

Grace had them stop and look through one of the stationdirectories to find where the next escape pods were and if they were still available. All of the options in the Synnr quarters were either gone or non-operable.

"This doesn't look good," she said. "We have a couple options in the common areas, and the escape pods in the Apsyn quarters. But fighting our way through there would be suicide."

"I'm not ready to die today," said Zac. "What's our next option?"

Crowze racked his brain for ideas. No escape pods. No other convenient cruisers. They were stuck on the station until help arrived. So where could they hole up?

"The control room." It came to Crowze in a flash. If they could get to the control room they could barricade themselves there and probably wreak havoc on the Apsyns.

"That's going to be almost as dangerous as getting to one of the escape pods," said Grace.

She was probably right, but there wasn't a better option.

With the destination in mind, they took off. And just as predicted, Apsyns stood in their way. The first one fell quickly, one Apsyn against a bonded Synnr unit. It was no fight at all.

The second Apsyns they met were more prepared. Two on three. Crowze, Grace, and Zac had more raw power, but the Apsyns had training. Zac was hit by a direct jolt of a spark and it sent him falling to his knees. Grace wouldn't stand for that. Though she was still figuring out how to control her powers, she was able to lash out with a mix of her spark and her fists and make short work of the Apsyns.

They were almost to the control room. Crowze could see the door. There were supposed to be guards, but they were gone. That was probably better for them all. Crowze didn't want to have to fight them off.

They were almost there. And once they were through the door they could barricade it. Maybe this hadn't been a terrible idea.

Crowze cried out as something sharp and fiery hit him square in the back. He fell forward and looked up to see Grace and Zac yelling before they returned fire to whoever had hit him. Crowze tried to turn over, tried to get to his feet, but he couldn't move past the pain. He tasted copper in his mouth and spat out blood.

Grace and Zac got their arms around him and pulled him into the control room before shutting the door behind him.

Crowze heard someone call for the med kit and it was all blurry after that.

***

Grace couldn't panic. There were Apsyns on the other side of the door and Crowze was bleeding. If she panicked, things would go from bad to worse. And Zac was right there with her, his hands shaking as he pushed them against the wound in Crowze's side. His face had gone pale, even paler than usual, and there was despair in his eyes.

What were they supposed to do? She had already dealt with one of her men being severely injured, she didn't want the other one hurt. Or worse. Thankfully, the healing cream had done its job on Zac and he seemed to be doing better.

But Crowze looked bad.

Really bad.

He was moaning quietly, little whimpers and groans coming out of him as she or Zac had to reposition him. But he didn't seem aware of his surroundings. He wasn't quite conscious. They needed a doctor.

No doctor was coming.

Grace looked around wildly and found the med kit hanging on the wall. She yanked it down and opened it, looking madly through it for anything that might help Crowze. Zac followed her instructions as best as he could and they got the wounds covered, but a few of Crowze's bandages immediately soaked through with blood.

Not the time to panic. Not now.

The med kit had a small blanket inside of it and she and Zac covered up Crowze, trying to make him as comfortable as possible.

Zac was running his fingers through Crowze's hair and he looked up at Grace. "He'll be fine." It was false confidence, but Grace appreciated the effort.

"Of course he will," she agreed. "He's too tough for anything else to happen." She couldn't say death. She couldn't even think it.

"Do you know what to do with any of those computers over there?" Zac nodded towards the control station. Normally there should've been two people in the room monitoring the maintenance of the space station. Grace didn't know where they were, and she was happy they hadn't had to fight them off.

Grace was no computer expert, but she was probably better equipped than Zac to deal with

Zulir technology. She had been raised in this world, after all. But she didn't want to step away from Crowze's side. What if he got worse? What if he asked for her?

She forced herself to stand. She would only be a few feet away. She could still look over and see both him and Zac. And if they were very lucky, maybe she could send out a distress call to the Synnr ships that were supposed to be coming for them. Or maybe she could do something that would screw with the Apsyns. That was almost as good.

There were various blinking lights and screens along with more keyboards than she knew what to do with. It took Grace a few minutes to make sense of anything. And even then she was sure she was only looking at the most basic functions of the control room. It appeared that most of the space station was automated. It didn't require Zulir intervention to keep functioning. That was good in normal times. Probably for the best when it came to the safety of people in the station. But today she didn't care about most of those people's safety. She wanted to make them decidedly unsafe.

A few random presses on the keyboard brought up information about where people were on the station. Unfortunately there was no convenient marking between Synnr and Apsyn. She could see a group of people congregating in the Apsyn quarters, but she had no way to know if they were actually Apsyns. She saw a command that could cut that section of the stationoff from the rest, but if the Apsyns had rounded up Synnrs over there, she did not want to take away their main escape route.

She could also see a report that showed more than one third of escape pods had been ejected. She hoped that meant most of their people had gotten away. But again there was no way to tell.

Something was messing with the communications. She couldn't find a way to send a call from the space station to a Synnr ship. Maybe she was just looking in the wrong place, or maybe the Apsyns had planned to cut them off. But basically what it told her was the controls were useless.

She quadruple checked to make sure that the doors into the control room would remain locked for as long as the control room had power, but that was about all she could do.

She wanted to collapse in failure. She was supposed to be a soldier, a warrior. She was supposed to be able to keep her people safe. And here she was stuck cowering in the middle of the space station, hoping for rescue before one of the men she loved died.

Grace choked back a sob she was not going to cry. Not now. Not until this was over.

Or maybe never.

Something tugged on her spark.

Grace's head jerked to look at Zac. "Are you doing that?" she asked. It was kind of uncomfortable, like an itch she couldn't really scratch. She hadn't been aware of her spark before she bonded to Crowze and Zac, but in the hour or so since it had happened there had been a constant swirl and pull between the three of them. It hadn't been uncomfortable, even if it was new. Not until now.

"That's not me," Zac said. Then he looked over at Crowze. Their Synnr warrior opened his eyes and said something, but it didn't make sense to Grace, and she figured Zac didn't know what he was saying.

"I think he wants our spark," said Zac. "Maybe that will help him heal."

Grace had never heard of sparks working like that, but she was willing to try anything at this point.

She abandoned the control panel and came back to kneel beside Crowze. She and Zac held hands over Crowze's body, and then each of them took one of Crowze's hands. It took a bit of concentration to figure out what to do, but then she was sending her spark straight into Crowze, maybe even overloading him with power. She didn't know what was too much. She had to hope this was going to work.

Grace was starting to see black spots beside her eyes, and she hoped she wasn't sending away too much power. She didn't want to stop. Not until Crowze was awake and okay.

But when the banging started on the door, she feared she didn't have another choice.

Chapter Eighteen

Grace was holding on to Crowze's hand so tightly that Zac didn't want her to let go. So this time it was he who got up from Crowze's side and went to check the control panel. Luckily the cameras were still up and he didn't have to struggle through deciphering any of the commands.

"It's the Apsyns," he said. They were banging on the door, trying to get past the lock. They shot it with their blasters and tried to zap it with their sparks, but nothing seemed to make the door budge.

Good.

Grace stared at the door, as if the strength of her gaze alone would be enough to keep it closed. If she was doing something, it seemed to be working. With nothing else to do at the control panel Zac scrambled back to Crowze's side.

"Any idea how long it will be before backup comes?" Backup *was* coming. Zac wasn't going to surrender to despair or fall to the belief that they would be sacrificed for the greater good. The queen had promised that backup was coming. If she said it, it was true.

He had to believe that. The second he gave into an inch of doubt they were dead.

But Grace looked grim. Her lips were set in a thin line and her eyes narrowed. "It all depends on how strong the Apsyns are. And whether they have anyone surrounding the station."

"Don't we have cameras looking outside?" Zac asked. He didn't know exactly what they could see from the control room, but that seemed like something that would make sense.

Grace let out a frustrated breath. "Whatever is disrupting the ability to send messages is also disrupting the outer cameras. We're flying blind."

Not what he wanted to hear. Zac grabbed back onto Crowze's hand and sent his spark into the man. Crowze sighed, as if it was giving him some level of relief, and Zac sent a little more. Was his spark exhaustible? Or could he keep sending as much power as he wanted? Already he was feeling a little bit weaker and he figured he knew the answer to that question, but he could give more. Especially if it meant Crowze would be better faster.

This was what he had signed up for. Being bonded to two warriors. It could just have easily been Grace lying between him and Crowze. And with this action by the Apsyns there was no way the war was going to be stopped. What would he do now?

Would he be expected to fight alongside his Matches? It was intolerable to think of being separated from them, to think of them being in danger while he sat safely on Aorsa. But he was no fighter.

They would have to deal with that later.

Eventually the banging on the door stopped. The Apsyns had given up. For now.

Zac couldn't let himself relax. He didn't know how much time had passed since they had barricaded themselves in the control room, and he figured they should probably be keeping track of that. Backup had to be coming soon. He hoped.

Several minutes later an alarm blared, loud enough to make him wince and make his ears ring.

"Life support system compromised," came a computerized voice. "Oxygen levels dropping. System reboot imminent. Station will fall back to secondary life support in fifteen minutes."

"That doesn't sound good," Zac yelled, over the still blaring alarm. "Do you think the Apsyns did something? Or is this somebody blasting their way on the station?"

"No way to know," said Grace. "But there should be some life support suits in here somewhere. We need to put them on. I'm not about to trust the secondary system under these circumstances."

With time counting down both he and Grace had to leave Crowze for a moment to find the suits. They were hidden away, locked in a small closet, but they found four suits, all of them in perfect condition. They were bulky, and a garish neon green. But they weren't as big as the spacesuits he had seen astronauts wear back home. They reminded him more of what he'd seen racecar drivers wear. The fabric felt kind of flimsy and the air tanks were small, but Grace didn't seem to doubt what they had.

He and Grace worked on getting Crowze into his suit first. It took some tricky maneuvering, pulling the legs up over his torn clothes and trying not to damage the bandages that he was wrapped in. He made a sad sound and Zac's heart ached, but they had to get him into the suit. It took nearly 10 minutes. But once it was done, Zac and Grace were able to put their own suits on with no trouble.

Grace scrambled back over to the control panel.

"What are you doing?" Zac asked. Now he sounded weirdly mechanical, his voice coming through a speaker behind his helmet.

Grace typed something on one of the keyboards and let out a curse. Zac looked down at the bulky gloves they were wearing and winced in sympathy. It could not be easy to type accurately wearing the gloves. But she didn't take them off. "I'm trying to see if there's anything I can do to fix life support. And I want to make sure that secondary system is going to work."

That sounded like the job of a trained technician, but Zac kept that thought to himself. No reason to knock Grace's confidence.

Grace yelled and smacked the desk before pushing off of it and coming back to Crowze and Zac.

"No luck?" he asked.

"No."

He let it lie. They were doing their best. They just had to wait for help to come.

And then there was more banging on the door. This was much fiercer than anything the Apsyns had managed. Zac didn't think the door would hold.

"Can we see who it is?" he asked.

"The Apsyns destroyed the camera," said Grace. A sense of calm infused her words. She was ready for battle.

Zac hadn't magically become a fighter in the past few minutes, but he and Grace had to keep Crowze safe until he could get medical care. They had to do their best to stay alive. Zac let his wings unfurl. It was weird how his clothes didn't interfere with them, but he couldn't think about it for long. He could spend hours studying his wings when they were safe. Right now they just had to be a tool.

Grace unfurled her own and Zac stopped thinking about his wings. Hers were a thing of beauty, full of greens and purples and strings of gold. He wanted to touch them, but he wasn't sure if it would hurt. Considering they shared a spark now, he didn't think it would. But again, they would have to save the testing for later.

By unspoken agreement they dragged Crowze behind the control panel where he would be more concealed from any fighting. It wouldn't matter if Zac and Grace fell. But Zac didn't want to get caught in thoughts like that.

But at least if he was going to die, he was going to die with the people he loved.

And death would be better than capture by the Apsyns. He knew exactly what they could do to a person. He didn't want to be their lab rat again.

The door shuddered a final time and Zac braced himself for the fire that was to come.

But as the smoke cleared and the first soldier stepped through, Zac almost fainted in relief.

Synnrs.

***

What was going on?

Where was he?

Why did everything hurt?

He was being moved. Crowze was sure of that much. Something jostled him from side to side and he groaned. He was wearing something heavy. Why? Before he could think to ask much more, blackness swallowed him.

Time passed. Possibly. Crowze couldn't be sure. Something bumped him again and woke him up. Was he awake? He could make out the outlines of people and he wasn't scared. Friends? His spark danced and flowed inside him, mixing with the power from Grace and Zac. It hadn't been a dream, then. Their bonding. It had really happened. They were really his.

He tried to open his eyes. Were they open? He wasn't sure. Lifting his lids was too much effort. Someone said something to them, but he couldn't make sense of the words. He was going to be okay? How could they know that. The pain was almost too much to bear. Had he been stabbed? Set on fire?

Darkness again.

The queen was in trouble. He had to save the queen.

It startled him out from the blackness. He tried to sit up but hands shot out all around them to keep him down.

More yelling. And when he tried to move again there was something on his chest holding him down. Had they strapped him in place?

"The queen," he gasped out. "The queen." He couldn't make a full sentence. Couldn't put thoughts to the words.

"She's fine," a feminine voice. Grace. His. He turned toward her, or he tried, but the restraint holding him in place wouldn't let him. He babbled something out, but it didn't make sense. He didn't even know what syllables he had made.

Then there was a masculine voice, saying something. Zac? Was Zac okay? Crowze could feel their sparks again and he tugged on them. Wanting the comforting closeness that they could provide. Power flowed through him, and the pain was almost gone.

Was that their spark? Or was it the prick of something on his arm? He couldn't think enough to figure it out.

Much later—he was sure it was much later because he could actually think—he began to wake up. He wasn't moving anymore. And bright lights overhead told him he was in some kind of hospital or med bay. Were they back on Aorsa already? Now he could remember that they'd been on the space station. There had been an attack. He had been injured.

Where were Grace and Zac? He tried to move and found he was still strapped down, but he could move his head. No one was in the room with him, and he was hooked up to more than a dozen machines. How long had he been out?

Where were Zac and Grace?

He needed them right now. Needed to see them. To know they were okay. He would've sacrificed his life for them in a heartbeat, but it was all for naught if they hadn't made it.

One of the machines started to beep, but Crowze barely paid attention to it. Where were Zac and Grace?

There. He could feel their sparks enter him right before Grace, quickly followed by Zac, burst through the door.

They both looked like they had fought armies to stay by his side. Deathly pale, dirty, with matted hair and torn clothes. But they were smiling at him. That was good. Smiling was good.

Even more of their combined spark flowed into him. Crowze couldn't manage words, but he could smile back.

There was a final burst of spark sent into him and then Grace's eyes rolled back in her head and she collapsed to the ground. Crowze let out a yell of shock as Zac followed immediately after.

Someone rushed into the room. He wanted to help. Wanted to say something. But he slipped back into unconsciousness before he could figure out what was going on.

Chapter Nineteen

Grace knew where she was by the smell. Clean, a bit bleachy, and very antiseptic. A hospital. How had she gotten here?

She remembered someone banging on the door of the control room. She remembered the blaring siren as life support failed. And then everything got a bit blurry. She hadn't been injured. Of that she was certain enough.

So why was she laying in a hospital bed?

She looked to each of her sides and saw Zac and Crowze both lying down. She couldn't quite reach out and touch either of them, and she wished they were all in one big bed together. But that probably didn't work in a hospital.

She wiggled her fingers and toes and rolled her head from side to side. Everything seemed to be working, even if it felt like she'd been lying here for quite some time. Had she fallen into a coma? No. She was pretty sure that hadn't happened. But she would like to know how long she'd been lying here.

And what had happened since then? Had the war started? Were she and Crowze about to be sent off into battle as soon as they could walk? What would a war between a planet and its moon even look like?

She didn't know. She was a bit afraid to find out. There had not been a full out war between the Apsyns and the Synnrs in a very long time and things had surely changed since the last one. Maybe this war would be fought in space. Maybe it would be a war of infiltration and skirmishes. Or maybe it would be some sort of convoluted game between the queen and the prince, each of them vying for power over the Zulir.

She didn't know. She was concerned about what it would mean. But for the moment she put the concern aside. She had both Crowze and Zac and she was going to appreciate that for as long as she could.

Crowze let out a sound and started to move. She looked over and he smiled at her.

"How are you feeling?" Crowze asked, as he stretched his arms above his head. She could see his muscles ripple under the thin clothing he was wearing and she wanted to touch him.

Later, she assured herself. Soon there would be plenty of time. "I'm a little stiff, but I'm doing okay." It was nothing a few stretches wouldn't fix. Or a nice walk around the building.

Crowze's smile grew filthy. "Give me a little time and I can be a little stiff too."

"Don't have fun without me," Zac added. Grace turned and saw him watching her from her other side.

"I love you both." It slipped out and Grace almost smacked her hand across her mouth as if she could call the words back in. Sure, it had been a bit joking when she said it, but she meant it. She had never said those words to a partner before. But they were real. "I love you," she said to Crowze, and then turned and repeated it to Zac.

Zac's smile was ecstatic and she could feel a burst of Crowze's spark flow through her. She didn't know a spark could be happy, but his was. Really, this laying in bed situation without both of them touching her was not working for her. Grace scooted back until she could sit up. It wasn't perfect, but it meant it was easier to look at her men. After a moment Zac and Crowze did the same.

"What happened?" Zac asked. "How did we end up in the hospital?"

"I'm not sure." She felt fine. And there were no bandages or scars to indicate an injury. She didn't see anything on Zac either. Crowze had lost a bit of color and did have a few bandages, but that was to be expected.

"You gave me too much of your sparks." Crowze's face was serious and he glared at them for a second. "You need to learn to control that."

"I won't regret it if it's what saved your life," said Grace. Beside her, Zac agreed. And she didn't point out that she and Zac had been doing pretty well for only being bonded for a matter of hours. It took some people months to master their sparks. And Zulir grew up learning what to do.

"I don't want you to die to save me," Crowze insisted.

"We're all safe now, and no one is talking about dying," Zac insisted. Grace glanced over and saw the serious look on his face. He wasn't a fighter. He had never been in battle before. Was it going to do some sort of lasting damage to him? She hoped not. But if he needed help to recover mentally from the ordeal, she and Crowze would make sure he got it. He was theirs to protect.

"How long have we been here?" Grace asked. Maybe Crowze would know. She didn't know if either of them had been awake yet.

"Only a day," Crowze answered. "The doctor said he just wanted to wait for you and Zac to wake up before letting us go."

"What about the war?" Zac asked. "Kidnapping the queen, or trying to, has to be a big deal. I can't imagine she's happy about it."

"I don't know," said Crowze. "No doubt the queen is talking with her council. And no matter what happens we will find out soon enough."

Zac still had more questions. "What about the three of us? We're a bonded unit, right? Don't units fight together? I think I remember hearing something about the powers being wonky if we get separated."

Grace and Crowze shared a serious look. Zac was right. Bonded units, especially newly bonded units, needed to be near one another for their sparks to work.

Near was a relative term. It could be a hundred feet or ten miles, it all depended on the unit. But she, Crowze, and Zac had not been apart at all since their bonding. They had no way to know what their range was or if it would grow. "We'll figure it out soon enough," said Grace. She didn't want to drag Zac into war with them, but she didn't want to consider giving up her career either.

"I'm not a fighter," Zac said, confirming what she already knew and making her fear that they had rushed into this thing too soon. "But I'm ready to kick Apsyn ass. I'll fight with you if we can stop those assholes."

Grace couldn't stop the smile that formed on her face if she tried. Maybe it was bravado. Maybe Zac would change his mind. But they would have that conversation later.

Her stomach rumbled. "I'm going to go in search of some food. Are you guys hungry?"

"You can do that?" Zac seemed surprised that she would get out of bed.

"What? " Grace was confused.

"Back home—on Earth," he corrected, "nurses and doctors get mad at you if you get out of the hospital bed."

"Earth is weird," said Crowze. Grace agreed; she was happy to have been born on Aorsa.

Grace got out of bed and was happy not to be dizzy or in pain. Crowze seemed to be right. She had depleted her newly found spark, and now that she'd rested she was feeling fine.

"Are you going to leave your wings out like that?" Crowze asked.

Grace looked over her shoulder and was shocked to see the burst of color behind her. She hadn't realized that her wings were out.

Some Zulir liked to keep them out at all times while others mostly kept them hidden. It was a personal choice. And Grace wasn't yet sure what she would want to do. It took some getting used to. She tried to pull them in for a moment, but they didn't seem to want to go away. It didn't matter.

"I think I'm going to stretch them," she said. Better to make it sound like a choice.

Grace left the room and took off down the hallway. Surely there had to be food somewhere. She wasn't familiar with this hospital. She assumed they were in Osais, but there was really no telling. She turned down another hallway and almost ran straight into her mother. "Grace!" her mom said. "Wings!"

Grace's cheeks heated and she was strangely embarrassed. She knew she shouldn't be. It was perfectly natural to keep her wings out like this. But it felt like she was confessing to something. These wings were a manifestation of the love she had for Crowze and Zac. Anybody who looked at her would see a part of them. But was that really so bad? No. "Mom, what are you doing here?"

Her mother looked at her like she had just failed a school exam, disappointed and a bit exasperated. "Visiting my daughter in the hospital."

"Right." That made sense. Grace might've had issues with her family at times, but she had never doubted her mother's love. "I was looking for some food for me and Crowze and Zac."

"I should've known that one Match would never be enough for you," her mom said with a grin.

"Mom," Grace protested, mortified to realize she sounded like an upset teenager. "No, we are *not* talking like that."

"Too soon to tease?" her mom asked.

"Way too soon." Grace wanted to make it off-limits, but that would just make things worse. But still, she needed at least a week to adjust to this. Everything was new and a bit fragile—not their love, but the bonds they were creating. They needed time to settle into things.

"So should I pack up your stuff and send it to Crowze's estate? Or will you be coming home to get it yourself?" This time her mom did not sound like she was teasing.

Grace's brain misfired and she couldn't quite summon a correct thought. "What?" Crowze's estate? Her stuff? Was she moving in with them?

Many bonded units lived together. And she didn't want to be separated from Crowze or Zac. But wasn't this really soon?

Her mom took her arm and started leading her down the hall, saying something about a cafeteria. Grace followed behind while her mind raced. She tried to wrap her thoughts around all the way things had changed in the past few days.

She was going to need a little more time.

***

Crowze's house was finally a home.

Maybe it was a bit ridiculous to think something about such a massive estate. And Crowze would never dare say that to his family. But while they all lived on the estate together, their lives were completely separate. He wasn't sure the last time he had spoken to a member of his family for more than a handful of minutes.

Now we had Zac and Grace with him. Officially living with him. He was so happy he could dance. Of course, then Zac or Grace would fret and send him back to sit on the very comfortable chair they had set up right outside his main closet. He had offered to help. They were rearranging things to accommodate their own clothing, and they insisted that his help wasn't needed.

But from the way they were handling some of the fabrics of his finer suits, Crowze wished they would just let him take over. He didn't consider himself fussy, but some fabrics were delicate and he wanted to make sure that his things were taken care of.

"If you think any harder you're going to give yourself a migraine," Zac said, grinning at Crowze through the open door. He folded one of Crowze's jackets and put it into a drawer. Crowze winced as it got caught with part of the sleeve hanging out.

"You know I love you, but my clothes are delicate." He didn't care when he got blood on his uniforms, when that fabric stretched and ripped. That was what it was made for. But not this.

"Do we?" Grace asked. She set down some of her own clothing and came to stand by Zac. "Do we know that?"

Zac looked up at her with a smile. "I don't know that we know that, he's never said it before."

They had to know. Crowze had never once hidden his emotions from either of them. He wouldn't have pursued thek in the first place if he didn't think there was a possibility they could fall in love.

But had he really never said it?

"I'll love you even if you destroy my suits," he assured them and tried to remind himself that suits could be repaired and replaced.

Grace stalked towards him and sat beside him. There was plenty of room on the chair. She leaned in and gave him a kiss before pulling back. "Even if we destroy your suit?" she asked.

"Yes," Crowze said solemnly. But he didn't think the other two were taking it as seriously as he did.

When he looked past her he saw Zac had come over. Zac leaned down and kissed him even more soundly than Grace had. Crowze tried to hold on to him, to keep him close. Both Zac and Grace had been treating him like he might fall apart with a bit of rough use. But his body was crying out for rough use. With both of them. Vigorously.

He had to convince them he was completely recovered.

And now seemed like just the time.

Or it would've been, if his communicator hadn't beeped. It was a call Crowze had been expecting. And if it had been anyone else he probably would've ignored it. He hoisted himself up from the chair and walked to the other side of the room. Zac immediately took his place and Grace crawled into his lap, kissing him. Crowze's cock twitched and he had to look away. He did not want to get aroused while speaking to a superior officer.

He engaged the call. "Major Ozar," he greeted.

Oz's mother returned the greeting. "How are you recovering?" she asked.

"Almost back to hundred percent." Really, if he could crawl into bed with Grace and Zac everything would be perfect again. But he wasn't going to say that to the major. "Grace and Zac are doing well too." Their stay in the hospital had been enough to scare him, but it had mostly been due to exhaustion and depleting their sparks. They had no lasting effects. Crowze would have a scar for the rest of his life.

"I'm happy to hear that," she said, and it sounded true. "When can we expect you back for training? I can give you and your unit the rest of the week, but no more. Soon we will need everyone we can get."

It was a question that Crowze had been dreading. Not because he didn't want to return. And he was sure that Grace was just as anxious to get back to training. But now Zac was bound to them. Was he ready to endure everything that came with being part of a bonded unit? Was he ready for war?

Major Ozar seemed to sense the direction of Crowze's thoughts. "Zac is Matched to a pair of warriors," she said. "Clearly he's tough. And while the three of you are a unit, we aren't going to throw him into the middle of battle. You know we like to accommodate these things."

It was true. At least as far as Crowze knew. Bonded units were rare enough that they needed to be used carefully. And they were strong enough that almost no one was a Match for them. It didn't mean that he didn't want to keep Zac and Grace as safe as he could. "Is it war then?" It had to be. Right now all the people in charge were probably just finalizing the details.

"It's looking that way," said the major. "And this won't be a war like we've ever seen before. I've never seen the queen so upset. And the prince..." She trailed off. "He thought she was weak. She will show him Synnr strength. And I fear that we are looking at total annihilation if we want to end this thing. "

It chilled Crowze to the core. He didn't understand the Apsyn way of life. The way they treated humans and other non-Zulir was abhorrent. But was the only way to stop them really to kill them all? He hoped it wasn't the case. He didn't know if the Synnrs could come back from that kind of destructive rampage. "We will be ready next week," he said.

He ended the call and took a moment to himself. But only one moment. He and his Matches had one more week before they had to go back and get ready for the danger to come. He was going to take advantage of every minute he could.

Chapter Twenty

Grace and Zac had their stuff all comfortably situated in Crowze's closet. Well, *their* closet now. She didn't let herself get hung up on thinking about whether or not this happened too fast. They were a bonded unit. A Match. Battle tested, and compatible in all ways. She didn't need to worry about the rest of it.

And Crowze's closet was more than big enough for the three of them.

So was his bed. She didn't think she would ever get tired of that. Of lying in between her two men, feeling their chests rise and fall against her skin. She could spend forever just sitting there.

And that seemed like a much better use of her time than the alternative.

"I don't think they really want me there," said Grace. She knew the way the humans looked at her, knew that they, at best, had conflicting thoughts. When they had met she had been terrible to them. She'd had to be. She didn't want to intrude on a celebration.

"Luci would not have invited you if she didn't want you there," said Zac. He squeezed her shoulders, offering a bit of comfort. "It's a birthday party. You'll survive."

Would she? "They don't really like me." It felt so juvenile to be complaining like this, but it was true. Why would they want her?

"You were invited. That means they want you there. And if it's absolutely terrible, you can leave. That's the beauty of it happening on the estate."

He had a point there. Crowze had agreed to host the party. So really, if things went terribly, she could run and hide. Not exactly the attitude of a decorated Synnr warrior, but not everything was a battle.

"I don't see why anyone would object to you being there," Crowze said. And the way he was looking at her sent a shiver down her spine.

Crowze got up close and covered her mouth with his. Thoughts of a birthday party, worries about the other humans liking her, all of that dissolved under the onslaught of sensation. Crowze's lips, his tongue, was just what she needed. She let herself fall into the kiss, surrendering to him and the sensations he gave her.

But she had to breathe. Sometimes she forgot how when she was kissing her men. She pulled back, panting, and Zac was right there to take her place. Grace watched the two of them for several moments, struck by the beauty of her two men wrapped up in an embrace. But she wasn't going to be left out.

She sank down, tracing her fingers over Crowze's body and then tugging his pants down to reveal his thickening cock. She licked and kissed, swirling her tongue around him and getting him so deep in her throat that she almost choked. There was something powerful in feeling him harden all the way in her mouth. She was doing this to him. She and Zac.

Forever wouldn't be long enough to find all the ways to share pleasure with these men. And then Zac bumped against her from behind and Grace turned to him.

She wouldn't want him to feel left out.

He felt different in her mouth, but she felt no less powerful, especially when his hips jerked and he made a desperate sound of pleasure. She could keep doing this until he came, until she tasted him emptying into her mouth. She didn't think it would take much. But she didn't want this whole encounter to be over so soon. It didn't matter that they had a lifetime. She wanted to cherish every minute.

Crowze must've pulled away from Zac at some point. She'd gotten so caught up in the taste of Zac but she'd stopped paying attention. But then they were repositioning themselves on the bed so Zac was bent over her with Crowze positioned between her legs. Where had her pants gone? It didn't matter. She didn't care. Now would be a great time to figure out how to make her clothes dissolve with a thought. Not that that was ever going to happen.

And there was Crowze's tongue, plundering her, making her squirm.

She had never been so satisfied before, so complete. Between these two men, their bodies all joined together.

Joined together in one way. But they could have more.

With a curse Zac pulled away, and Grace didn't even recognize the sound that came out of her mouth.

Zac bent down over her and captured her mouth in a rough kiss before pulling away. "You like the feel of us in your mouth?" he rasped out, his voice rough and filled with lust. "Like when we fill you up?"

Grace moaned. There were no words. Nothing but sensation.

Zac looked down at Crowze and silently communicated something to him. Crowze pulled away from her for a moment and when he came back he didn't use his tongue. Instead his fingers were coated with something cool and slick. Lubricant.

"Were going to leave our mark on you, make it so you never forget what this is like." Crowze's fingers dipped into her as if he was moving by Zac's command. He stretched her, preparing her like she'd never been prepared before.

"What are you—" It ended on a gasp as Crowze stretched her even further.

"Can you open for us? All three of us together, you squeezing us tight while our cocks rub against each other?"

Grace could barely imagine it, and from the rough moan that was pulled out of Crowze, he wanted it just as bad as she did.

"Yes." She would beg if she had to. Both of them inside her? They'd done it once before, but not like this. She wanted to figure out every way this could work. Them inside her. Them inside each other. They could figure out if they could use their sparks during sex. Maybe even get her a toy or two. There was no end to the possibilities. But Grace wanted more right now.

And Crowze agreed. "Now," he said.

Crowze entered her first, the lubricant helping him slide all the way inside. It was good. It was always good when it was one of them. But then there was Zac, nudging his way inside of her and taking it from good to amazing. The stretch was almost too much, but her body yielded to them, prepared, ready. Two cocks deep inside of her. Her men.

And then they started to move. They had to go slow. Maybe one day this would be something fast, something that could absolutely destroy her in the best way possible. But not today. She was connected to both of them as deeply as people could ever be connected. She could feel the cocks sliding against each other, and she saw Crowze's wings burst out of his back. His control was slipping.

She loved it.

His cock started to vibrate; he was close to the edge, it wouldn't take much.

But it was enough to send her over, rippling around both of them and crying out in pleasure.

Zac and Crowze followed, emptying themselves inside of her and breathing heavy.

Grace drifted for a while after that, just enjoying the feeling. She felt a bit drunk, but nothing that alcohol could ever give her. This kind of drugging could only ever come from her two men.

"I would have never expected you to have that mouth on you," Crowze said after a few minutes.

Grace had to agree. But she couldn't speak in complete sentences yet. She didn't know how Crowze managed. Still, she made a sound of agreement.

Even in the dim light of the room, she saw Zac blush. "You two bring it out of me," he said.

"We should." Crowze sounded smug. "You're ours."

Grace liked the sound of that. Zac and Crowze were hers. She was theirs. They were each other's. It didn't get better than that.

She kissed them both, her body sated. But when it came to the two of them she would always want more.

Chapter Twenty-One

It wasn't anything like an Earth birthday party.

Okay, that wasn't exactly true. There was music, and cake. Well, the Synnr version of cake, which was close enough. And a dozen humans. And even more aliens.

Luci's birthday party, in its own way, was a sign of how their lives had changed. But it was a good change.

Zac was happy. Really, really happy. And he was glad to see his human friends smiling and dancing and playing in celebration of Luci.

Everyone was there. Oz and Emily, Solan and Lena, Jori, Ax, a bunch of Synnrs that Crowze didn't recognize, and all of the humans that had been rescued from Kilrym all those months ago.

In the center of the festivities was a dance floor and Luci was shaking and spinning and laughing, and no one was safe from being summoned into her orbit for a song or five. Zac had already taken a turn, but he was laughing as Crowze and Grace were shooting him alarmed looks while Luci made them spin. Zac left them to it. His tough Synnr warriors could handle it.

"You look happy," said Joel, coming up to him and handing him a drink.

Zac was thankful for hydration. It was hot outside and he had worked up a sweat. "I am," Zac agreed. All the issues he'd had before diving headfirst in with Crowze and Grace turned out to be unfounded fears. No one cared that he was bi. No one cared that he was with two people. They just cared that he was happy. If they cared at all.

He didn't know if it would ever have worked out on Earth. And he was still sad some days when he remembered that he would never go back to his home planet. But it got easier. Being with Crowze and Grace, having friends among the humans, carving out his life on Aorsa all made it more of a home.

Someone called Joel away, but Zac wasn't alone for long. Luci came up to him, breathing heavily, her cheeks pink with exertion. Her eyes sparkled and she couldn't stop smiling. "You were holding out on me," she teased. "Maybe I should go get two Synnr boyfriends of my own." She grabbed Zac's drink out of his hands and gulped down the final sips.

"I was drinking that," he said with a laugh.

"It's my birthday. I can do what I want." And then she stuck her tongue out at him.

Zac could warn her off pursuing two people. It had worked out well for him, but it took more work than a single partner. But he would be a hypocrite to say that. Now that he had Grace and Crowze he couldn't imagine a better way.

Luci's smiling face soured as she looked past him. Zac turned to look over his shoulder and saw Jori dancing close to a Synnr woman. They swayed together with the music and he kissed her in a way that suggested they were far more than friends.

"Anything wrong?" Zac asked.

Luci had a crush on Jori. Everyone knew it. He wanted to offer her sympathy, but he didn't want to ruin her birthday party.

"No, of course not." Luci rolled her eyes, and she crushed the cup she had stolen from Zac in her fist. "I don't like Jori. He's way old. Like thirty or something. I am *definitely* not into him. No way. And he looks weird. So that's not happening." She gestured broadly as she spoke, wrinkling up her face as if she smelled something terrible.

There were about a hundred things Zac could say, and he couldn't settle on one of them. Luci had been through a lot the past few months. They all had. But she was still just a kid in a lot of ways. She had a bruised ego, and it was her birthday. Maybe she deserved to sulk.

Ax came up to them and wished her a happy birthday with a smile. Luci's eyes got wide and she grabbed onto Zac's arm, as if she was afraid that he would walk away.

Was there a problem with Ax? Had he done something? The man looked nice enough. Zac didn't know him well, but he was one of the soldiers that had been responsible for freeing him and his friends from Kilrym.

He saw Crowze and Grace on the dance floor and they were gesturing for him to join them.

But if Luci was feeling apprehensive, he didn't want to leave her to it.

Thankfully, Joel came up and joined them, so Zac pried Luci's hand off of his arm and let her be.

Dancing with them this time was different than before. Surer. Zac was no longer conscious of other people watching them; he didn't care who was looking. All that mattered were his two partners and the pleasure and fun that they could bring together.

Some things about Synnr life weren't bad at all.

It took a break from dancing a little later. "So is that Jori's girlfriend?" Zac asked casually. Crowze and Grace knew him better, they worked with him. He wasn't asking for Luci. Okay, that was a lie. He was definitely asking for Luci.

"Jori doesn't have a girlfriend," said Grace. "He doesn't do relationships. Just casual."

Crowze agreed with a nod.

Luci would like the first part, but was bound for disappointment with the second. But at least he had the information if she asked. She could consider it a birthday present.

Crowze kissed his cheek and then whispered in his ear. "There's a fountain just past the house. Meet us there."

"Isn't it rude to leave the party when you're the host?" Zac leaned against him and reached out for Grace's arm, pulling her close and kissing her. She melted against him. A few weeks ago Zac wouldn't have been able to do this. He wouldn't have been comfortable enough to kiss both his partners in front of everyone. Now he wanted everyone to know that they belonged together.

He let out his wings, the surest sign of a bonded Match. Let everyone else be jealous. They were his.

"It's your home now too, both of you," said Crowze. "I think that makes you both hosts as well."

Satisfaction zinged through Zac. His home. He liked that.

"No one will miss us for a few minutes," he said.

"Oh," said Grace. "This is going to take more than a few minutes." She kissed both of them and took off. A moment later Crowze followed.

Zac knew he should wait at least five minutes before leaving. Anyone who saw them would know what they were doing. Not that it mattered.

He lasted three and a half minutes. He headed down the path and was determined not to be stopped, but he heard something rustling in the bushes just off the path and he had to pause to see what it was. Especially when he heard a woman laugh.

It was Luci. Well, it was the back of Luci's head, and her arms were wrapped around a tall man. A Synnr, but he was mostly hidden in the shadows.

Was it Jori? Given what he'd just learned about the man, he didn't want him taking advantage. Besides, he would be a dick to abandon his date. He stepped forward, not sure what he was going to do, and the light shifted.

It wasn't Jori. It was Ax.

Well. That was unexpected.

But it was just a kiss. And Luci was old enough to decide what she wanted for herself. Especially on her birthday. But he would probably find out more later.

He stepped back and headed towards the fountain. When he got there Crowze and Grace were sitting on a bench, already embracing. Zac sat right down beside them and joined in.

He didn't know when his birthday was; he would probably have to figure that out eventually. But as far as he was concerned, Crowze and Grace were the best birthday present ever.

***

Did you like this story?

Please consider leaving a review at your favorite retailer.

And if you *really* liked this story, share it with a friend!

***

What to read next:

Soulless: Detyen Warriors

Available in ebook, print, and audio!

When a mission for the Sol Intelligence Agency gets out of hand, Sierra will need to use every skill she has and work with a mysterious alien warrior who awakens an unquenchable desire within her.

What's Next: Soulless

Can a man without emotions find his mate?
There's nothing left in Raze. No love, no hate, nothing but the duty that he owes his people. But when he meets a fascinating and tough human woman on a barren planet something deep inside comes back to life and for the first time in years he yearns for more.

Can she trust the ice cold warrior?
When a mission for the Sol Intelligence Agency gets out of hand, Sierra will need to use every skill she has and work with a mysterious alien warrior who awakens an unquenchable desire within her. He's cold and forbidding, but when he looks at her there's a fire in his eyes that opens up a whole world of possibilities.

Two worlds collide...
The chemistry between Raze and Sierra is too hot to ignore, even if it should be impossible for a mate bond to form between them. They'll need to fight pirates, their people, and fate itself to be together. But it may already be too late for the soulless warrior and the woman he aches to claim.

Available in ebook, print, and audio!

Also by Kate Rudolph

Looking for something else? Kate Rudolph has a heart pounding collection or paranormal and sci-fi romance stories for you! Bundles, bears, audiobooks, aliens, and more. Check out your options in the list below. You can find out all you need to know at www.katerudolph.net.

***

Save with box sets!

Aliens. Shifters. Warriors. Mates. Get them all wrapped together in these special box sets. Save up to 30% off the price of buying the individual books, depending on the series!

Alien Outlaws: The Complete Series
Mated to the Alien Volume One (also available in audio)
Stealing the Alpha: The Complete Series (also available in audio)
The Mate Bundle
Detyen Warriors Volume One (also available in audio)
Detyen Warriors Volume Two (also available in audio)

Zulir Warrior Mates
Alien Warrior Romance

Kidnapped humans. Alien Warriors. Electric wings.

The Zulir Warrior Mates series brings you human heroines and heroes abducted from Earth who find love – and wings! – with the alien warriors who rescue them. *Also available in audio!*

Synnr's Saint
Synnr's Hope
Synnr's Spark

Mated to the Alien
Fated Mate Alien Romance

Detyens are doomed to die young if they don't find their fated mates.

Follow along as these mated pairs fight off aliens, corrupt dictators, prejudiced humans, pirates, and more! The books can be read or listened to in any order, though some characters show up in multiple stories. ***Select books available in audio.***

Pick a book and jump into the action today!

Ruwen
Tyral
Stoan
Cyborg
Krayter
Kayleb
Shayn
Braxtyn
Doryan

About Kate Rudolph

Kate Rudolph is science fiction romance author who lives in Indiana. She loves writing about kick butt heroines and the steamy heroes who love them. She's been devouring romance novels since she was too young to be reading them and had to hide her books so no one would take them away. She couldn't imagine a better job in this world than writing romances and sharing them with her fellow readers.

If you enjoyed this story, please consider leaving a review.

Keep up to date with what's coming soon, get access to exclusive giveaways, and hang out with Kate online in her Facebook group! Kate Rudolph's Detyen Dreamers is where Kate Rudolph fans can hang out and talk about the latest in alien romance.

www.ingramcontent.com/pod-product-compliance
Lightning Source LLC
Chambersburg PA
CBHW051652180726
48284CB00006B/1963